KANSAS CITY NOIR

KANSAS CITY NOIR

EDITED BY STEVE PAUL

Published by Akashic Books
©2012 Akashic Books

Series concept by Tim McLoughlin and Johnny Temple
Kansas City map by Aaron Petrovich
Cover photo courtesy of the Missouri Valley Special Collections, Kansas City Public Library, Kansas City, Missouri

Printed in Canada

ISBN-13: 978-1-61775-128-8
Library of Congress Control Number: 2012939264
All rights reserved

First printing

Akashic Books
PO Box 1456
New York, NY 10009
info@akashicbooks.com
www.akashicbooks.com

ALSO IN THE AKASHIC BOOKS NOIR SERIES

FORTHCOMING

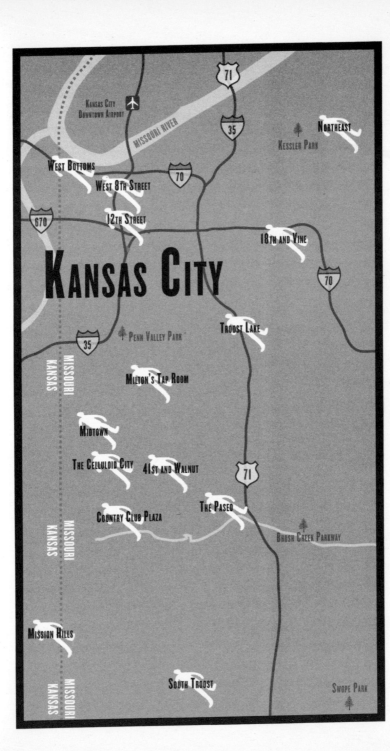

TABLE OF CONTENTS

PART III: SMOKE & MIRRORS

INTRODUCTION
Papa's Blues

I t was winter when a young newspaper reporter, recently back from the war in Europe, holed up in a rooming house in Michigan and turned his mind back to Kansas City.

He churned out a story of the kind he hoped one of the magazines would want. There was a murder. There was a mild-mannered newspaper man named Punk Alford. And there was an anguished, effete suspect who stroked a sword's edge as if it were . . . well, you know.

Whether the budding author mailed that early effort to the *Saturday Evening Post* or any other magazine is unknown. But the story was never published, so Ernest Hemingway's future reputation was spared embarrassment and his apprenticeship in writing continued a few more years.

Hemingway, of course, later penned some of the great noir ur-tales of the 1920s and '30s, notably "The Killers" and *To Have and Have Not*. Lesser known among Hemingway's fictional record are murky-toned stories such as "A Pursuit Race," about a wigged-out heroin addict, and "God Rest You Merry Gentlemen," featuring a castration, both of which share two significant things with the unpublished Punk Alford story—namely, an origin and a setting in Kansas City.

Hemingway was eighteen years old in October 1917 when he arrived in Kansas City from a Chicago suburb to become a reporter at the *Kansas City Star*. For the next six and a half months, before he decamped to join the ambulance service in Italy, Hemingway discovered, while chasing ambulance surgeons and cops, what we still know: the streets of Kansas City are paved with dark tales aplenty.

Kansas City is a crossroads. East meets West and North meets South here. Since its settlement in the first half of the nineteenth century, Kansas City has represented a place of opportunity, optimism, and ornery behavior. It outfitted travelers and dreamers on the Santa Fe, California, and Oregon trails. It grew on cattle, grain, and lumber. It nurtured Jesse James, jazz, and gin-slinging scoundrels.

When I put out the call for contributions to this collection, I imagined we'd produce tributaries to a fictional stream that extends from nineteenth-century cowboy novels, through Hemingway's brand of gritty tales, and to the contemporary, unsparing visions of his successors. (For a taste of period Kansas City pulp at its peak, try finding—it's not easy—a copy of *Tuck's Girl*, a paperback novel published in 1952 by another onetime *Kansas City Star* reporter, Marcel Wallenstein.) I deliberately failed to define "noir" to prospective contributors. As previous anthologies in this series have shown quite effectively, the term represents a big tent. So here you will indeed find serial killers, moral turpitude, and police detectives at work. But you are just as likely to encounter quieter tales of inner turmoil, troubled reflection, and anxiety. The heart in stress can lead people to unpredictable and midnight-blue places.

In "Cat in a Box," Kevin Prufer's veteran detective/protagonist is on the trail of a killer while his own body threatens to change the course of his life and career.

In Nancy Pickard's "Lightbulb," a woman climbs deep into regret and guilt over an old memory. Pickard's story also negotiates the long shadow of Kansas City's racial divide, as does Linda Rodriguez's tale of a widower trying to maintain his life's order in a time of upheaval and collision.

Some stories within evoke real places and people, though just a reminder—this is a collection of fiction, not history. In "Come Murder Me Next, Babe," Daniel Woodrell, master of Missouri noir, imagines a femme fatale who may resonate with Kansas City readers of a certain age. And in setting "Yesterdays" in Milton's Tap Room, Andrés Rodríguez imagines an alternate history for the much beloved bootlegger, bar owner, and friend to jazz, who died in 1983. (Milton's, a noirish bar if there ever was one, I add with great affection, also shows up as a touchstone in Philip Stephens's troubling and trenchant Midtown tale, "You Shouldn't Be Here.")

By contrast, Nadia Pflaum invents a barbecue legacy that may or may not sound like a real Kansas City institution. (We repeat: any resemblance to real people . . .) And Phong Nguyen steps into that nineteenth-century dime-novel current to imagine an episode from the earlier days of political machinist Jim Pendergast and his famous Climax Saloon.

Some stories take liberties with geography and specific places, which, of course, is the prerogative of fiction writers. Local readers can make their own gotcha lists, though I trust they will do so with a smile and nonetheless recognize their city's pulse reverberating in these pages.

First-time visitors to Kansas City usually note with surprise the greenery and the winding, hilly topography of our sprawling, two-state metropolitan area. Yet even the City Beautiful foliage and suburban finery can hide crime and lives of moral weakness, as Grace Suh displays in "Mission Hills Confidential."

Tourists and locals alike love their sports here, their slow-smoked ribs, their shopping, and the gab that goes on at neighborhood bars. Walking on the wild side is a long tradition here too, evidence of the full range of Kansas City's human condition. Our lineup of fine writers explores that condition in numerous and compelling ways. Through wintry chill. Through moonlit mystery. And often, befitting our literary and musical heritage, through singing the blues.

Steve Paul
Kansas City
June 2012

PART I

HEARTLAND

MISSING GENE

BY J. MALCOLM GARCIA

Troost Lake

F ran's at night school studying for her associate's degree. I don't feel like watching TV so I get out the knife one of the interpreters gave me in Kandahar and start throwing it at the wall. He said he got it off the body of a bad guy who blew himself up laying an IED in the road, but I think he stole it off one of our guys, because it's a Gerber and it doesn't look like it was in any explosion. The terp could throw it and stick it every time. I'm not that good, but I throw it at the wall anyway. I can do it for hours.

I was a contractor over in Kandahar. Electrician. Worked there for twelve months. When my year was up, I flew home to Kansas City and took up with Fran and a couple of months later moved in with her. Mr. Fix It, the soldiers called me. Did some plumbing too. A little out of my league, but at two hundred tax-free grand a year I was more than willing to say I could do anything. I got used to the noise: mortars, sniper fire, return fire, .50-calibers, AKs, generators grinding all night, guys living on top of each other telling dead baby and fag jokes. Awful quiet now that I'm back. Behind Fran's house, I hear buses turn off Prospect and onto 39th Street, drone past and slice into the night until I don't hear anything again. The knife helps. I like the steady repetition of tossing it. The precision of it. Like fly fishing. Gene understood. He fought in Korea.

The trick with the knife, I told Gene, is you got to establish a rhythm. You do that and the silence becomes part of the flow and the *plink* the knife makes when it enters the wall interrupts the silence, and the small suck sound it makes when you pull it out, and then the silence again until you throw it, again and again.

Right, Gene said.

Next day

This is the third week I haven't seen Gene at Mike's Place. Out of all the regulars, he's the only one missing.

Melissa isn't here but we all know where she is. A public defender, Melissa has a court case this afternoon. I overheard her tell Lyle yesterday she would be working late. And Lyle? He may have a job painting or installing a countertop or a new floor or fixing someone's shitter. What I'm saying is, Lyle's around. He's a handyman. He'll be in later, as will his buddy Tim.

Bill's here. He's retired from working construction and basically sits at the bar all day drinking up his disability. And Mike, of course. It's his bar. The floor dips and the stools wobble, all of them, and the top of the pool table's got a big slash in it and someone walked off with the cue ball, but it's a good place—cheap, and it's only a couple of blocks from Fran's.

Then there's Gene. Or was. He drove off is how I look at it. Flew the coop, as they say. Well, that's it. I'm leaving too. Montana is what I'm thinking. I've been considering a move for a while. I mentioned Montana to Gene. He thought it was a good idea.

Wide open, no people, he said.

Absolutely, I said.

I'll tell Fran tonight.

Evening

What's on at seven?

Golden Girls reruns.

Oh.

You've had beer.

I was at Mike's.

Well, you missed my mother.

Oh . . . yeah?

Yeah. It's all right. I wasn't expecting her.

Fran's mother does that; drops by without calling. She's divorced and bored. Good thing Fran was here instead of me. Her mother nags me when Fran's not around. She knows I'm not going out on many jobs. I've told her we're okay. I earned a bundle in Afghanistan. She thinks I should have stayed another year and made even more.

I'm going to Montana.

Montana?

Yeah.

When?

I don't know.

Oh.

I play solitaire, spreading the cards across the blanket of our bed. I tell Fran not to move her legs beneath the blankets and disturb the cards but she does anyway.

Why Montana?

It's wide open.

Fran doesn't look up from her book, *The General and the Spy*. A man on the cover wears an open red tunic and some tight-ass white pants a real guy'd never wear. His skin's the color of a dirty penny and he has no hair on his chest. A woman's got her hands on his stomach, ready to rip into those pants I bet.

Fran folds the corner of a page, closes the book, and wipes tears from her eyes.

Nobody cries over those kinds of books, I tell her.

Montana?

I'm thinking about it. Gene's missing.

Who?

A guy I know.

Fran goes, Let's change the channel. Then let's talk.

Go ahead. Change it.

I changed it last time.

What do you want to watch? I ask.

I don't know.

She picks up her book and puts it down again. We stare at the TV, the remote between us.

Next day

Bill sits beside me at Mike's, buys me a beer. Crass old fucker Bill. Bald as a post and bug-eyed. He's always hunched over and rocks back and forth and makes these sick jokes about his neck being so long he can lick his balls like a dog. Deaf as Stevie Wonder is blind.

Hey, Bill, Tim says.

What you say? Bill asks.

Fuck you, Bill, Tim says.

What you say?

Tim laughs. Laughs loud and talks loud like we're all deaf as Bill. He sits at the end of the bar where Gene always stood, wipes his hands on his sweatshirt and jeans. Tim works in a warehouse in the West Bottoms. Refrigeration parts. Something like that. Comes in grimed in grease and oil. Starts at five in the morning and works all the time, weekends too. With jobs the way they are, is he going to say no when his boss offers him extra hours? I don't think so. Not with paying out child support to his ex.

His money being so tight is why he killed his dog's puppies. At least that's how he explains it. The dog, a brown and white mix between this and that, had a litter of seven. He put six of them in a pillow case and dropped them in Troost Lake. Then he shot the dog. Easier than getting her fixed. I stopped sitting next to Tim when I heard about the puppies.

Every time I think of them, I'm reminded of these Afghan laborers in Kandahar. One afternoon they found some puppies when they were collecting trash. A trash fire was burning and they threw the puppies into the fire. You want to hear some screaming, listen to puppies being barbecued. I hear them now. I ball up my fist and right hook my temple once, twice, three times, waiting for what

I call *relief pain* to wrap my skull and take their shrieks out of my head. Tim and Bill look at me. I open my fist.

Fucking mosquito, I say and smack the side of my face again.

Big-ass mosquito, Tim says, still looking at me.

It's strange seeing him in Gene's spot at the end of the bar. Gene never sat, just stood. No matter how cold, he always wore shorts, a T-shirt, and a windbreaker. Brown shoes and white socks. Legs skinny and pale as a featherless chicken. Wore a cap that had the dates of the Korean War sewn in it. He told me that Kansas City winters didn't compare to a winter in Korea.

I saw frozen bodies stacked like cord wood covered with ice, Gene said. Some of them I put there.

It got cold in Afghanistan too, I said.

I remember one time when this truck driver got to Kandahar in December. Brand new. Just off the bus. He was so wet behind the ears I had to tell him where the chow hall was. He kept rubbing his hands together and I pointed out the PX where he could buy some gloves. He went on his first convoy an hour later. This guy, he got in his rig, took off, but realized he was in the wrong convoy. He turned back to the base and approached the gate fast because he was out in no man's land by himself. You didn't approach the gate fast. You didn't do that. But he was scared. Some Australians shot him five times with a .50 cal. I mean, he was obliterated. They had to check his DNA to figure out who he was. Less than two hours after I showed him the chow hall, I saw them put his body pieces in bags.

Evening

Fran tells me what I'm planning is called a *geographic*. Moving to get a new start somewhere else in the mistaken belief you'll leave your bad habits behind is how she puts it. She studied psychology last fall and thinks she can pick apart my mind now.

I mean it. I'm gone, I say.

She goes, When you decide to do it, just go. Don't bother telling me because I'm not going with you. Men have left me before. I survived. I'll survive you. Leave before I come home. Make it easy on us both.

I will, I say. I can do that.

Okay, she goes, okay.

Next day

Just me in here this afternoon.

What's the latest on Gene? I ask Mike.

Haven't heard a thing, he says.

Mike has owned Mike's for ten years. He was in a band, got married, and had a kid. In other words, time to get a real job. So he bought the bar and named it after himself. He's divorced now, sees the kid every two weeks, plays gigs occasionally, and runs this place. Says if he ever sells it, the buyer will have to keep the name. Years from now nobody will know who the hell Mike was but his name will be here. A piece of himself nobody will know and can't shake off. That's one way to make an impression.

I first came to Mike's by chance. I used to drink at another bar on the Paseo but one night it was packed. After Kandahar, I couldn't handle crowds, so I left. On my way home, I stopped at Mike's. Some lights on but barely anyone in it. I had a few beers and came back the next night. Two nights in a row and Mike figured he had himself a new regular. He bought me a beer and said his name was Mike. We shook hands. Sealed the deal, as they say.

I met Fran here. She was shooting pool by herself. Bent over the table, her ass jutted high and round against her jeans, and any man with a nut sack would have known that if she looked that nice from behind she'd be more than tolerable face-to-face. And, if she wasn't, so what with an ass like that. But she was fine all the way around.

She had light brown hair and a determined look. My glance moved down past her chin and rested on a set of perky tits that pressed just hard enough against her T-shirt that my imagination did not have to strain too hard to know what would be revealed when she undressed. I asked to shoot pool with her and we got to chitchatting. One thing led to another is what I'm saying.

I'm not sure when I noticed Gene. I just did. I remember seeing this old man at the end of the bar and thinking how solitary he looked, how he was off in his own world. He had one of those faces that sort of collapsed when he didn't talk, mouth and chin merging into a flat, frowning pond. When he took off his hat, the light shined on his bald, freckled head. He'd still be standing in his spot when I left a couple of hours later, the same bottle of Bud he had when I first came in half empty and parked in front of him. He barely said a word to me in those days. Just nodded if we looked each other's way. But then as I began showing up every night, he started saying hello and I'd say hello back.

Evening

Fran and I drop our plates onto the crumb-graveled carpet for our beagle to lick. Partly chewed pizza crust, orange grease. Slobbered up in seconds. I reshuffle the cards.

I'm going to sleep, Fran says.

Say what?

Turn the TV off.

I'm still up.

Turn it down then.

It's not loud.

Please.

But it's not.

Shhh.

I shut off the TV, go out to the living room. I sit in the dark fingering my knife. The way Gene has vanished, an eighty-year-old man. I can't help but notice the empty space at the bar. Like a radiator turned off. All that dead air, dead space.

Funny what you learn about a guy after he's gone. For instance, Tim and Lyle said that Gene would come to Mike's at eleven in the morning. He would stay all day and apparently be pretty toasted by the time he left at closing. Really, he never seemed messed up to me. Maybe he kicked in and drank like a horse after I left.

One night, Gene told me he had taken his landlord to court. It wasn't clear to me why. I believed him, and whatever the reason, he made it seem like he'd won the case. After he disappeared, Bill told me Gene lived in his car. There never had been a court case or a landlord. Bill had put him up in his place but not for long. Said Gene wandered around the house with nothing on but his skivvies. I couldn't have that, Bill said. Not with my wife in the house and the grandkids coming over. I don't care if he is a vet.

Next day

Hey, Lyle, Mike says.

Mike, Lyle says, and takes a seat near Tim. He has his hair roped back in a ponytail and wears an army fatigue jacket that hangs well past his hands. His feet dangle off the bar stool and tap the air. He reeks of pot.

I was just getting ready to leave, Tim says.

No you're not, Lyle says.

He turns to me.

What's going on? Working?

Absolutely, I tell him. Staying busy.

You were in Afghanistan, weren't you? How was that?

Good. It was good.

That's good.

Actually, it was kind of crazy.

Crazy can be good, Lyle says, and he and Tim laugh.

Mike, I'll have another, Tim says.

I notice Melissa come in the back door.

Hi, Melissa, Mike says.

Hey, Melissa, Lyle says.

Melissa, what's up, Tim says.

Hey, Melissa says.

She sits next to Lyle and orders a Bud Light and a shot of Jack. She has on heels, gray slacks, gray jacket, and a white blouse.

Won my case, she says. Got him off.

Since none of us know who she's talking to, we all nod at the same time. Melissa smiles. She starts talking about the first time she came in here as she always does. I don't know why it bears repeating. I mean, I've got the story memorized. But she likes telling it. Maybe it gives her a sense of seniority. After Lyle she has been coming here longer than the rest of us. Like it makes her feel she belongs is what I'm saying.

It was just before closing, Melissa says. Mike and Lyle were shooting pool. Gene was in his usual spot. She remembers Mike saying he was about to close. Then he let her stay and the four of them had beers and got stoned after Mike locked up.

Gene got stoned? I say.

Yeah, Melissa says.

I hadn't heard that part before.

Evening

Fran tells me that instead of doing a geographic, I should go with her to visit her sister in St. Louis. It would be cheap, she says. No hotel or eating-out expenses.

Sounds okay, I say.

Did you order a pizza?

Not yet, I say. I'm tired of pizza.

What do you want?

I don't know. Shit, what's up with all the questions?

Fran goes into the kitchen. I hear her making herself a drink. I try calling Gene. I gave Gene my cell number one night. He called me a few times before he disappeared but I could never make out what he was saying. He had a sandpaper voice that came at you like radio static. What's that? What's that, Gene? I'd say, and then he'd hang up. I'd call him right back but he'd never pick up. He doesn't pick up now. I get one of those female computer-generated voices telling me to leave a message. I'd like to talk to Gene, I say, and hang up.

Next day

Anybody hear anything about Gene? I ask.

Lyle shakes his head. Melissa and Tim look at Lyle and shrug.

Getting to be awhile, Lyle says.

Yeah, awhile, Mike says.

I shout in Bill's ear and ask him what he knows. Well, he says, speaking like he's got a mouth full of cotton, I spoke to one of his sons in San Antone. Yes, San Antone it was. Gene gave me his number when he stayed with me. An emergency contact, he had said. Well, let's hope this isn't an emergency because Gene's son wants nothing to do with him. One of those kind of deals, if you know what I mean. Still a lot of water under that bridge, I guess. Anyway, I told his son, I just want you to know your father is missing. We haven't seen him for the longest. Maybe he's headed your way. But his boy said again he wanted nothing to do with him. What can you do?

He doesn't expect an answer and I don't give him one because, well, what can you do? Melissa, Tim, and Lyle go out back to smoke. Mike steps into the kitchen. Bill stares at his glass. I tell him that today for no good reason I was reminded of this private, a young gal. We got mortared and she got all messed up. She lay on the ground, her right arm ripped to shit like confetti. Some medics put her on a stretcher and got an IV in her, and her shirt rose up exposing her flat stomach and full tits and despite all her screaming I thought she was beautiful. I went over to see if I could help and she looked at me wide-eyed and said, Am I going to die? No, I said. You're fine. You're going to make it.

Do I know if she did? No, I don't. That bothers me.

What you say? Bill says.

Evening

I call Fran from the union hall on Admiral Boulevard, shouting above the traffic noise of cars backed up overhead in the tangled mess that is I-70 and I-29 looping around one another. I only worked a few hours this afternoon, I tell her. I stuck around for something else to come up but nothing did. Can you pick me up?

Okay, she says.

By the time she gets me, I'm pissed off. Pissed I had only four hours of work today, pissed I couldn't get a ride home, pissed I had to wait around until Fran got off her job at Walgreens to get me. I was 360 degrees pissed off is what I'm saying.

I get in the car, ball my hand into a fist, and press my knuckles against Fran's right temple. She tilts her head away and I keep pushing with my fist until her head is against the window and I feel the vein in her temple pulse against my knuckles.

Stop it, you're hurting me, she says.

Next day

Mike, I'll have another one, Melissa says.

She's dating this gal, Rhonda, a school teacher. I don't know how old. Younger, I'd say by the look of her in a photo Melissa passed around. I don't care that she's gay. I mean lesbian. She corrected me one time. Men are gay, women are lesbian. Okay. What do I do with that bit of knowledge? Keep my mouth shut is what I'm saying.

Melissa talks about how nice it is to be involved with a woman who doesn't trip when Melissa has to work late. Doesn't ask a thousand questions to make sure that nothing is wrong. It's nice to be with someone who's an adult, Melissa says. She says that a lot. Nice to be involved with an adult. Like she's trying to convince herself that it's nice. Like maybe the confidence of her lover makes Melissa wonder what she's doing.

I'm going home, Tim says. Make some dinner.

What're you going to have? Lyle says.

I don't know.

What you say? Bill says.

Fuck you, Bill, Tim says, and he and Lyle laugh. It's not as funny as the first time he said it. It's starting to get old but I can't help smiling a little.

Gene and I had dinner together one night. I met him in the parking lot behind the Sun Fresh Market off Southwest Trafficway. I didn't know then that he was sleeping in his car. Just ran into him there and he asked me if I was hungry. Come to think of it, I said.

A bunch of clothes were heaped in the backseat of his station wagon. An old rusty job with wood paneling peeling off the doors. He had rigged a towel to take the place of a window that would no longer roll up. Laundry day, he said, explaining away the clothes.

We drove out of the parking lot to Mill Street and followed the curve into Westport to a little joint called The Corner. Some bums who might have been hippies years ago stood on Broadway wiping down car windows at a red light while the drivers waved them off. Gene and I sat down and a waitress cleared our table. I ordered a burger. Gene had the meatloaf special.

The Corner closed not long after that. A big *For Rent* sign hangs above the front door along with the name of some real estate company. I went by it the other day and noticed the table where Gene and I had sat surrounded by other empty tables made all the more empty by the emptiness of the place.

Evening

Fran's mother sits with me in the kitchen. Her perfume gives me a headache. I stare at her hair all puffy and piled up on her head and bleached so blond it's almost white. She twirls the lazy Susan with a finger, touches the corner of her mouth, and then goes back to spinning the lazy Susan, her finger skating along on a film of lipstick she rubbed off.

What's it taste like, your lipstick?

Why would you want to know? What kind of question is that for a man to ask?

I don't know, it just came to me, I want to say, but don't. One night, I was walking to the shitter and mortars started coming in. We were always being mortared. This is the real deal, baby! someone yelled. And then, the blasts lifted an eighteen-year-old private into the air, tossing him backward like a rag into all this dirt and noise and smoke; his blood sprayed over my face. I can still taste it.

Where's Fran? her mother says.

School, I say.

Have you thought of going back to school?

No.

Is it your plan for Fran to do all the work while you sit around? Fran's mother says. Have you thought about being more than an electrician?

No, Mrs. Lee, I haven't.

Well, it shows.

I apply a piece of Scotch tape to a corner above the cabinets where the wallpaper is peeling.

Fran's mother gets up and walks to the sink. I listen to the linoleum creak beneath her shoes.

When do you plan to clean these? she says of the dishes. Or are you waiting for them to pile up to the ceiling?

I throw the tape down and face her. She steps back, a little aren't-I-clever smirk on her face, and I turn the hot water on in the sink and pour in some soap. I find a sponge beneath the sink and start wiping down a plate. My fingertips turn white from squeezing the plate so hard. A littler harder and it would break. I want to feel it break but I ease up; put the plate in the wrack. I start cleaning another one.

You two should get married, Fran's mother goes.

I keep washing the plate.

You're living together, she says. Not having a job hasn't stopped you from doing that. Married, you'd at least be official. It would show responsibility. Now wouldn't that be something?

I rinse the plate, set it in the rack. I lean on the sink, arms stiff.

I'm leaving, I say.

You're leaving. Where you going?

Montana.

Montana. What are you going to do in Montana?

Work.

Work. Work here for a change. You think some cowgirl is going to put up with you?

I raise my hand before she says anything more. There's this nasal termite sound to her voice that chisels into my head. I press my fingers against my eyes. My neck feels hard as a tree trunk.

Fran's mother stands beside me. I ignore her, work on another plate. She runs a finger over the dishes in the rack and shows me a spongy speck of pizza crust glued to her fingertip.

You can't do any better than that? she says.

I smash the plate on the edge of the sink and throw the jagged piece still in my hand against the wall. Fran's mother steps back, her eyes betraying panic, her finger still poised accusingly, and I grab her finger with a fury that fills me with a terrible heat and force it back until she kneels, screaming. A pasty white color washes through her face when the bone breaks, and I feel something break in me and I keep pressing back on her ruined finger, until the bone tears through the skin and into my palm. Her eyes swell like something wide and deep rising out of the ground, bubbling tears, and her screams take on a new level.

I let go of her hand and jam my knee into her solar plexus and put all my weight on her chest. She gags and spits up whatever she ate this morning. I rise up and then drop my knee into her chest, and her neck and face go all purple, and I do it again until I feel ribs crack under my knee. I sink into her chest and down to her spine like falling through ice. Blood geysers out of her mouth and then her eyes roll back. Her tongue lolls out of her mouth like a slug and I smell her bowels. I push myself off her and sit at the table. The silence is almost as loud as her screams. I focus on the hum of the refrigerator. White noise. I take up my knife. My hands shake and at first my throws are way off. Then my breathing steadies and I get my rhythm back and throw it once, twice, three times into the baseboards, the refrigerator humming behind me.

Next day

Rhonda's not answering, Melissa says, looking at her iPhone. Why isn't she answering?

The front door swings open.

Hey, Heidi, Mike says.

Hi, Mike, Heidi says.

She plops down beside Lyle, her mop of curly red hair flouncing on her shoulders. The two of them started dating not too far back. She tends bar here on the weekends. Has two kids. Their daddy dealt drugs and got busted. Lyle sells drugs, but hasn't been busted. I think she can do better. I bought books for her five-year-old daughter. I figured she'd appreciate that. Little picture books. But she started seeing Lyle and I quit the book thing. Maybe books weren't what I should have been giving her in the first place. But I was with Fran so books seemed appropriate. Neutral. Not too over the top is what I'm saying.

I force a smile at Heidi but I don't strike up a conversation. I'm not really here. Yesterday seems far away and today doesn't feel like today. I hear Heidi and Lyle talking but it's all background noise to Fran's mother dying. That's how I look at it. She died. She was in the wrong place at the wrong time. Something snapped inside me and she died. It was not me who killed her but something working through me I can't define. That something left me afterward as suddenly as it had come on and I almost fell asleep in the kitchen throwing my knife. But then the old me came back and I knew I had to clean up the mess left by that something else.

I carried Fran's mother into the garage and put her in the

trunk of my car and covered her with a blanket. Finding a mop, I returned to the kitchen and washed the floor. Back in the garage, I looked for a box of five-, ten-, and twenty-pound weights Fran had bought at a yard sale when she got it into her head she was going to exercise. Dust and cobwebs covered the weights and clung to the hair on my arms, and I felt each hair released when I wiped the cobwebs off.

I put some rope and the weights in the trunk and drove to Troost Lake. Clouds sealed the sky so that no stars shone. I followed Troost Avenue to the turnoff into the lake, and the road narrowed and wound around the lake and my car lights skimmed over the oil blackness of the water and the wet stone walk where old men fished during the day. I parked the car under some trees, opened the trunk, and trussed Fran's mother up with the rope. She wasn't too heavy even with the weights I'd wedged beneath the rope. I held her and listened to what I thought was an owl. Shadows rose and dipped above me and then darted away and I could only assume they were bats. I waited for the owl to stop calling. In the vacancy left by its silence, I rolled Fran's mother down a hill and she splashed into the water and was absorbed into its darkness leaving only ripples that spread into nothingness.

Evening

When I'm with Fran, I think of her mother. I don't need that. I sit alone in the kitchen while Fran sleeps and punch my temples until my head feels like it will explode and thoughts of Mrs. Lee shatter into bits. I think of Gene and what he would say.

The last time I saw him, he was standing in front of a Church's Chicken near Gillham Plaza and 31st Street. It was hot and the wind blew trash and some napkins were pinned against Gene's knobby white knees. We said hello and he offered me a ride but I told him I had my car. I'm getting some coffee, I said.

When I went back outside, he was still there. I looked at him and he gave me a knowing wink like we were both in on something no one else would understand. I don't know what that might have been. But I'm thinking now he might have done some awful things in Korea besides killing gooks and letting their bodies freeze, and I think he saw in me the ability to do some awful things too, and then Fran's mother died and he was proved right. I'm just saying. I don't know. Gene didn't say and I never saw him again.

Next day

Okay, Mike, I'm outta here, Tim says. After one more.

I'll do one more too, Mike, Lyle says.

What you say?

Fuck you, Bill.

Lyle and Tim stand and walk outside to smoke. Melissa follows them tapping a number into her iPhone. Heidi looks at me and smiles. She asks Mike for a cigarette. Watch my purse, she says. Then she goes outside too. Mike puts two bottles of beer on the bar for Tim and Lyle. I wave him off when he looks at me. I feel all hemmed in. The beer congests me. It's difficult to breathe.

I'll pay up, Mike, I say.

Evening

In bed Fran rolls over with her back to me, her head on my right arm. I grit my teeth. Her touch sends shock waves through me and I get all jittery. I edge away from her. She says she has called her mother a few times but no one answers. It's not like her, she says. Her mother doesn't have an answering machine so Fran is going to go by the house in the morning.

That settles it. I'm out of here. When Fran leaves for work I'll be right behind her but headed in another direction. It will still be dark. I'll take 39th to Broadway and hang a right by the Walgreens and drive into downtown. A few blocks east, I'll see the glow from the Power & Light District keeping the sky open like an illumination mortar, and I'll cross the Broadway Bridge and get on I-29 north until I reach I-90 and then it's a direct shot west to Montana and wherever.

I feel my arm falling asleep beneath the weight of Fran's head. I curl it to get some circulation and realize I could choke her no problem. I drop my arm and slide it out from beneath her head and punch my temples with both fists until the pain overwhelms my thoughts.

I kick off my blankets; get my legs out from under the sheets. I long for a breeze. I imagine Fran's mother at the bottom of Troost Lake. I think of Tim's puppies and then I think of Kandahar and of other things I've seen. My head throbs. I shut my eyes against the room closing in on me, get up, and go sit in the kitchen. I find my knife, hands shaking. I start tossing it but can't establish a rhythm.

I drop the knife, think of Gene and of dead Koreans calling to him. I imagine he is sitting in his car miles away parked beneath a streetlight unable to sleep. Moths bounce against the windows. Flies strike the windshield. Beetles scuttle across the hood. I tell him that when I was a boy, my friends and I would drop grasshoppers into empty trash barrels and then we'd scream into the barrels and listen to our voices ping-pong against the sides like shrapnel, crumbling antennae, wings, legs. We'd pluck the grasshoppers out barely alive and bury them. I see them now, their jaws working furiously, filling with dirt. Hear the crunch-scrape of seeking mouths sucking air.

CAT IN A BOX

BY KEVIN PRUFER
Country Club Plaza

At last the cat fell asleep and, because Armand still could, he drove his police-issue Crown Vic through the Plaza, down Main Street. He took a left on 47th, slid past Latte Land then Pottery Barn, past Barnes & Noble and Gap Kids, then left again. Three fat men stood outside a fake Irish bar and laughed while the snow came down, but Armand drove right past them too, over the bridge at Wornall and left again, to Ward Parkway then Main then 47th again.

Around and around he drove while the cat slept in the cardboard box beside him.

Sometimes Armand's legs felt numb. Sometimes they tingled, as if he'd exercised too hard the day before, or a dull ache would curl up his thighs and settle around his hips. He knew he shouldn't be driving.

It was two days before Christmas. He'd seen the 280,000 colored lights blink on at seven p.m., during his first pass, while the cat meowed plaintively and scratched at the little air holes he'd cut in the box. Still driving, he unwrapped a sandwich, tremblingly swallowed cold coffee.

After a while the stores closed, their windows dying away in the gloom. A pretty girl turned the key on Burberry's and hurried to her car. The cat slept soundly again.

The restaurants went next, spilling their drunken yuppies onto the snowswept pavement where they fished in their coats for car keys or looked into the reflected Christmas lights in each other's eyes.

Armand drove in circles, listened to slush part beneath his wheels.

Once, he stopped the car and tilted the seat back and closed his eyes, but he didn't sleep. Instead, he concentrated on his fingers, willed them to open and close, played them awkwardly over the steering wheel, two taps of the ring finger, then the index finger, then the pinky, though they ached too. They were harder to control today than even ten days ago.

He'd given himself one more week. One week of driving, of East Patrol, of holding his coffee with both hands to conceal his tremor. Then he'd tell Jackson, who already knew something was wrong. And then he'd tell Balls, who would want his gun and his car keys, who would want his badge and his clip, who would nod gravely and say, "Armand, I don't know what else I can do." And there'd be a retirement party at Lew's and, after that, he'd end up drinking with Jackson and Rorkisha at the Cigar Box as long as their babysitter would allow, and then he'd drink alone or go home where, slowly, slowly, the disease would finish him off.

But he wasn't going to feel sorry for himself.

The Dollmaker had driven through these snows, smiling as the final stragglers exited the bars, slid into their cars. The Dollmaker had sucked on his Camel Menthol, peered through someone else's window, smiled, smiled, smiled.

"That cat," the boy had told him four nights before, "she get into everything. Everything." He held it to his chest, rubbed its chin. He was maybe twelve or thirteen, said his name was Lamar. "Where'd you find her?" he asked, not looking at Armand, no, looking at the cat, stroking it behind the ears while it stretched and purred. "You so thin," Lamar whispered to the cat, "you a thin little girl."

And Armand wasn't sure how much to say, what to tell Lamar, whose mother wasn't home, whose mother danced at the Fantasy Ranch on Route 50 halfway to Sedalia, which was a euphemism for taking off her clothes for truckers rumbling along through Warrensburg, Lone Jack, and Kansas City, toward the great blankness of Kansas itself.

"You know how I can reach your mom?" Armand asked, but the kid shook his head, said she wasn't answering the cell phone, but she'd call when she got her break.

"Where'd you find my cat?" Lamar asked again.

Armand sat on the front steps beside the boy, looking out over Prospect Avenue, unsure of what to tell him. Kids made him nervous—he didn't have any of his own, though once he'd thought he would. But he liked Lamar, who lived in a neat house on a not very good corner of a bad neighborhood.

A patrolman found the third victim, Wilma Perrin, fifty-five, in a white Toyota Camry parked illegally near the east end of a construction site where Bannister Mall once stood. Satisfied that she was dead, he closed the trunk and waited for Armand and Jackson to arrive.

The woman's eyes were open and glittered white in the street-lights' glare. Her teeth also glittered behind the sad grimace of rigor, her face tight and strange and pale. She probably hadn't been dead very long, though it would be hard to tell because of the cold.

She looked a lot like the little doll the killer had slipped into her mailbox before anyone noticed she was missing, a neatly sewn, three-inch-tall plump doll in a pale blue dress and tiny boots. The victims all looked too much like their dolls. The Dollmaker had studied them carefully, gotten the wardrobes just right, the freckles and the jewelry.

With the end of a pencil he carefully peeked under her collar at two thick welts. He'd choked her, but he didn't kill her that way. He'd choked her to have fun. Probably after he gave her the injection, as it was taking effect.

Sodium thiopental takes some time to work, maybe two, three minutes. So, first she became dizzy, then her eyes closed, her muscles going momentarily rigid, then slackening, loosening. Completely limp. Maybe he brushed hair out of her face. Then he choked her for a while. Then he straightened her collar to hide the welts. Then he probably followed up the first injection with another, this one phenobarbitol, to prolong the effect.

And then he'd loaded her into the trunk of the Toyota Camry—all this flashed before Armand's eyes quickly as he sat on the stoop with Lamar and the cat. He placed her lovingly into the trunk of a stolen Camry and drove her through the snow, down Hillcrest, where he parked the car and disappeared.

Armand told none of this to Lamar. Nor did he tell Lamar that when he and Jackson finally got that trunk open again—it had frozen shut—it was not the dead woman Armand saw first. No, it was the cat—Lamar's cat—tired, hungry, and angry, sitting on the victim's chest. Armand looked at the cat and the cat looked at Armand. Its eyes glowed greenly in the darkness.

Then Armand closed the trunk once more, lest the animal escape.

"Where'd you find my cat?" Lamar asked again.

And Armand shook his head. "Crime scene," he said. "She was at the scene of a crime."

Armand thought about all this as he drove around and around the Plaza, watching the last bars close. Through the windows, he could see waiters mopping floors, flipping chairs upside down atop the tables.

The cat mewed in the box beside him. When he turned onto Wornall, he heard pellets of food roll around.

From behind him came the long low moan of what might have been a cold wind. And the snow fell like a million little white angels in the night.

"Here's what we do," Jackson had told him, when they finally got Wilma Perrin to the morgue and the Toyota to forensics. "We put a tracker on the cat, then we let it go. The cat leads us straight to its home and there's our crime scene." He laughed, like it was joke, but it wasn't. And after a moment he said, more seriously:

"That cat got in the car at the same time Wilma did, to stay warm. And cats know how to get home."

Armand was thinking it over. The fact was, they had three victims. Three little dolls and three dead bodies. But no crime scene. The Dollmaker clearly hunted victims away from their homes, picked them out of crowds, met them in shopping malls or movie theaters, followed behind them on highways, cornered them in unfamiliar territory. He knew them well, had watched them, probably photographed them so he could make their dolls.

And somehow he subdued them, injected them, played with them, loaded them in the trunks of cars, drove them elsewhere still, to odd corners of the city, to out-of-the-way parking lots where, after hours, his victims slowly recovered, then—from cold, from thirst, bound and unable to move or call out—died. To think of it made Armand tremble, made him hold the steering wheel a little tighter.

This was where he was going: paralysis, then nothing.

As if he could calm the cat, he patted the cardboard box. "Good cat," he told it. "*Shhh.*"

Without a firm crime scene, they had no witnesses. If he knew where the victims had been abducted, he might find someone who had seen it happen, perhaps without realizing what he'd seen. But without witnesses, there was little to go on except the sodium thiopental and phenobarbitol, which led nowhere. And the dolls, which provided less than he'd hoped.

Armand was no cat person, but his wife had been, and when she died her cat had lived on another four, five years. And one day, when he'd brought the cat to the vet, the vet had offered to have it chipped. And this is how Armand came to know that lots of cats—all those adopted from the SPCA, for instance—came with a little microchip the size of a grain of rice embedded in the skin between the shoulder blades. And if this cat was chipped, that meant it could be scanned for the owner's address.

And with an address, they had something close to a likely crime scene. And perhaps there they'd find a witness.

It would be easier than following the damned thing through the streets of Kansas City, anyway.

It had begun with a strange, dull ache in his joints, as if he'd had too much exercise the day before, though Armand exercised rarely, and then only under pressure from his doctor or from Balls, his immediate supervisor, who insisted all of them, even sixty-five-year-old homicide detectives, achieve "a *level* of physical fitness." And quitting smoking hadn't been enough. And mostly laying off the drink hadn't done the trick, either.

But the ache remained, climbing up and down his legs, and then, a few weeks later, it was in his wrists. Sometimes it felt like handcuffs tightening over them. It was in his elbows, a sort of tingling pain, the sting of a bee. He'd grown unstable on his feet and, waking up in the middle of the night, had to hold the side of his bed to keep from falling while his legs attained their balance, while they caught up with the rest of him.

And his regular doctor looked concerned, as did the first specialist. And the next, and the third, a young Vietnamese woman who told him it was not going to get better, she was so sorry to tell him this. They could slow the process a bit, they would take an aggressive approach, there were a number of clinical trials going on right here at the KU Medical Center. "People live for years with this," she said, smiling, by which she meant that people *went on*, slowly losing the ability to move their arms and legs, unable, at first, to drive safely. And then to walk, or feed themselves, or change the channel, unable to do anything at all but lie in bed or look out the window at the snow, which swirled now around his car as he took another left, and another, driving around and around the Plaza, two days before Christmas, a cat in a box on the seat beside him. It was midnight now.

He hit a bump and something rattled in the trunk.

It would feel like being locked in a trunk.

* * *

Lamar was a good kid, a sweet kid. He wanted to know about the crime scene and Armand told him a little bit, that he'd found the cat in a stolen car.

"Cat gets into everything," Lamar said.

"What's its name?"

"Cat," Lamar said. "I thought you was dead," he said to the cat.

Armand smiled. Lamar stroked the cat.

"Was it that white Toyota?" the kid asked after a moment.

Armand felt his pulse quicken. He was waiting for Jackson to show up. But Jackson was going to be late.

"Yeah," Armand said. "You know the car?"

"Sure. Big Camry? It was parked right in front of the house for like three or four days and Cat pretty much lived underneath it. I had a feeling about that car. It didn't belong to no one around here."

"You see who was driving it?"

The kid thought about that. A Cadillac rolled down the street, stopped for a moment while the driver threw a can out the window, then emptied his ashtray onto the curb. "Yeah," Lamar said at last. "I think I seen him. He came and went sometimes."

"You remember what he looked like?"

"Did he steal the car?" Lamar asked.

"Yeah."

"Did he murder those people? The ones they finding in the trunks of cars?"

"You know about that?"

"I read the paper," Lamar said.

Lamar was sorry he couldn't remember what the guy looked like. He'd seen him several times easing the white Toyota into and out of that spot in front of his house, opening the trunk, hunting around inside. But he hadn't paid much attention.

Armand asked him lots of questions, told him to take a deep

breath. The kid looked like he was going to cry. "If you don't re-member his face exactly, do you remember if he reminded you of someone?"

But Lamar didn't know. "He was a white guy," he said, "kind of average. That's all. I didn't really *look*." And Lamar was really near tears now, he wanted so badly to remember, wanted Armand to think he was a good kid, a smart kid. And when his mother came home, he wanted her to know that he'd helped the cops with that big case, that he'd helped them catch the Dollmaker, but he couldn't remember anything except a white guy walking to the car every now and then, opening the trunk—he'd seen it through his bedroom window—closing it. A white guy in a yellow jacket. Or a white jacket. And a baseball cap.

And then the car was gone and Lamar had thought of it no more.

And now he was helpless. And he wanted his cat back for good. Armand said they'd hold on to it for a few days, bring the cat back home as soon as a vet could surgically remove the chip from its neck. Armand said they needed to keep the chip to preserve the chain of evidence.

But something bigger was nagging at Lamar, some detail, and after Armand left he kept thinking about it. He thought about it while he made himself mac and cheese, and while he curled on the couch to watch TV, then closed his eyes. He thought of it when, through the haze of sleep, he heard his mother unlock the door and shake him awake and put him in his own bed.

And he dreamed about it, the man in the yellow jacket unlocking the trunk of the car, dreamed the man lifted the trunk then glanced up at him. The man seemed to see Lamar's face pressed against the window. He smiled and waved. He was missing two fingers.

He had served on the KCPD for nearly forty years and still didn't want to retire.

And he'd worked 214 murders.

It was easy to say that most of those were mundane and

pathetic—a dead dealer, a gas station attendant who should have just handed over the cash, a gangster who thought he'd keep all the money and disappear. But the truth was, there was nothing mundane about any of them. Every dead hooker, addict, teenager was strange and mysterious to him. What had they been thinking? How did they become who they were, and why did they end this way, sprawled in the back of a Trans-Am, dead in the zoo parking lot, crumpled over their own front steps? What had their hemorrhagic eyes seen?

But these new bodies—these bodies in the trunks of cars, their little cloth images dropped in mailboxes—they hit him in a stranger place. They weren't mysterious at all, he decided, feeling the dull ache working his arms and legs, feeling his foot shift, unbidden. They'd died immobile too, injected and immobile. He was going to go like that—a prisoner in his own body, unable to move, unable to do anything at all. And when they closed the trunk on him for good, when the light failed—

Now, driving around and around in the Crown Vic, watching the snow pretty up the midnight sidewalks, he wanted to get out of the car and stab the Dollmaker. He hated him like he hated the quickly degenerating cells in his slowly failing brain. He didn't want to know the Dollmaker's story. He didn't want to know anyone's story.

He wanted the fucker dead.

When Lamar woke up, he was sure the guy was missing those two fingers. When he'd waved, his hand looked like a claw. Why hadn't he remembered that right away? Why hadn't he said it to the officer right away?

"You took the bus here to tell me that?" Armand asked, leaning back on his desk chair. He'd quickly put away the crime scene photos when the kid arrived, shoulders still dusted with snow.

Lamar nodded.

"Why didn't you just call?"

"I got no phone." He shrugged. The truth was, he wanted to see the station, wanted to come in person to make things right.

"And aren't you supposed to be in school?"

"I guess." The kid looked out Armand's office window, onto 27th Street. "I don't always go."

But Armand was smiling the whole time, so Lamar wasn't worried. "And you're sure the guy was missing two fingers, right?"

The kid nodded.

"The pinky finger and the ring finger?" Armand held his hand out, curling those fingers down so his hand looked like a claw.

"I'm pretty sure," the kid said. "I dreamed about it last night, but I'm pretty sure."

So what if the kid couldn't pick the freak's picture out of a photo lineup—"I don't really remember his face, just the hand," Lamar had said—what did it matter? How many perps were there in Kansas City with access to pharmaceuticals and missing those two fingers? It had to be William Steingart.

So Armand drove the kid home in his Crown Vic. And the kid asked again when he could have his cat back and Armand told him soon, soon. "The cat's fine," he said. "They're feeding him real good. Tuna and milk. It'll be fat and happy when you see it next. Just another day or so."

Steingart was a registered nurse, a sweet, lean, clean-cut bastard of forty-plus who smelled of Axe deodorant and something like playdough. When Armand asked how he'd lost the fingers, he smiled kindly, said he'd bet them away. "You should see what the other guy lost," he said. But when Jackson raised his eyebrows, Steingart demurred: "I fell, put my fist through a window. It was years ago. In St. Louis. Not such an interesting story, I'm afraid. But it doesn't slow me down any."

Steingart smiled through the whole interview, his chair tipped back. He was voluble, cheerful. He noted Armand's tremor, noted the scar that ran along Jackson's cheek. He told them about his wife, who taught fourth grade in Leawood. He told them about his car, how the heater was dead and he froze all the way here. "Anything to help you fellows out," he said.

And when Armand asked about how he was doing with his treatment, Steingart smiled, said he took it one day at a time. "You know, you're never really free of those thoughts," he said. "You just learn to control them. You learn not to act on them. To stay away from certain temptations. When they get too strong, I call my support team."

"Right," Armand said.

"I haven't done anything like that in years," Steingart said. "Not anything." But the guy's smile was weird, it was off, it was, Armand thought, hinky.

"You been driving a white Toyota Camry recently?" Armand asked.

Steingart thought about that one for a beat too long. "Nope," he answered.

"What about a '97 Honda Civic, dark blue?"

"I drive a Chevy Impala," Steingart said.

"You been hanging around near Bannister Mall at all?"

Again, Steingart appeared to think about it. "Bannister Mall's closed. There's nothing down there."

"What about Prospect Ave. and 67th?"

"Near Research Medical?"

"Yeah, near there."

"Now and then," Steingart said. "You know, there's a place I like to eat up there, Salaam Cafe."

Jackson crossed his legs, looked at Armand.

Armand grew flushed. His fingers tingled. His thighs ached. Then he looked out the window at the snow. "You kill those people?" he asked at last.

Jackson coughed.

"What people?" Steingart said, a faint half-smile playing over his lips.

"You know what people."

Jackson coughed again.

Steingart just smiled. He looked right into Armand's eyes and smiled and smiled. He wouldn't stop smiling, not even when Armand asked him again, not even when Armand got out of his chair, walked around the table, and grabbed him by the lapels and shouted into his face, "Did you kill those people? Did you kill them?"

And then Jackson was pulling him away, was saying, "Cool it, man. Cool it." And Steingart smiled that strange affectless smile.

And it was true, they didn't have a thing to hold him on. They couldn't even get a warrant on what they had: a kid who may have dreamed the missing fingers.

"I've had quite a day," Steingart said as he rose from his chair to leave.

"What?" Armand was still flushed, his legs unsteady.

"Real busy," he said, and before Armand could react, the man took his hand in his claw and shook it cordially.

Around and around Armand drove as the snow piled up. When he hit the pothole on the corner of 47th and Pennsylvania, he heard a knocking. Now and then, the cat scratched at the box. It was, Armand hoped, still a little drugged from its surgery. It let out a loud, deep meow.

The car rode low in the gathering snow.

Armand was thinking now about that fourth doll, the one Elizabeth Wallace's father found in the mailbox just that morning, not twelve hours ago.

"She was going to the mall," he said. "And she texted to say she was staying at Julie's. It seemed believable." The man was crying. He did not want to let go of the little cloth doll, the three-inch misshapen image of a pretty, plump redheaded girl of nineteen in jeans and a pink sweater.

"I'm so sorry," Armand said.

"But Julie never talked to her last night. She was never going to Julie's."

The man was twisting the little doll in his hands. Armand reached over, gently took it from him, slipped it into a little plastic bag.

"I'm sorry," he said. "I'll need a picture of her too. Something recent. Do you have something like that?"

Where had Elizabeth Wallace been going when she was seen last?

According to her father, she'd been headed toward Oak Park Mall.

Had anyone seen her in the mall?

Miller was on it. Melichar was on it. Nguyen was on it. So far, no one in any of the stores she frequented recognized her picture. At least not from the day she disappeared.

Gas stations? The post office? Blockbuster? Anywhere else she might have stopped on her way to the mall?

Nothing.

She'd gotten in her car and disappeared.

And now it was getting dark, the sky gone from gray to charcoal, and cold. Six o'clock, two days before Christmas. He'd been working since dawn.

Armand turned to Jackson. "I'm going to get a bite to eat, bring the kid his cat back." He'd made the cardboard box for the cat that morning. Once it had held reams of office paper.

Jackson nodded. He was on the phone, on hold. "You coming back?" he asked, covering the mouthpiece.

"Yeah," Armand said. "I just need some air."

"Bring me a sandwich," Jackson said. "And a Mountain Dew."

"Yeah," Armand said. "Got it."

"You're not thinking of visiting Steingart, right?"

"Right."

"Stay away from that," Jackson said. "I'm serious. We got nothing on him. If he did it, we'll get something on him. But you stay away from him for now."

"He did it."

"Stay. Away."

And he'd meant to do exactly that. He'd picked up the cat downstairs, carried it in the box through the snow to his car, placed it on the front seat. It mewed and scratched in the box beside him as evening continued to fall, as Armand drove up Broadway toward Lamar's house.

But all he could think about were Steingart's last words to him—*I've had quite a day . . . Real busy*—that strange smile playing over his wet lips, how he shook Armand's hand, the little squeeze he gave him, the way those three remaining fingers felt.

I've had quite a day, he'd said. "A busy day," Armand said out loud, his face grown flushed. The hot air blowing from the Crown Vic's heaters annoyed him. The cat angered him. Who the fuck did Steingart think he was? And in Armand's mind, the needle slid in, slowly, Elizabeth Wallace tipped back in the passenger seat of the blue Civic, eyes wide, a gun, perhaps, in his claw. He could hold a gun with three fingers; Armand had tried it.

Then he imagined Lacy Johnson, or Wilma Perrin, or Kaylee Sims—in and in and in went the needles while they cried, while their eyes rolled back and their arms went limp. Sometimes the needles went in just once. Sometimes, just as the women recovered, the needle went in again.

And what did they think as he closed the trunk over them, as they heard the car start up? As he drove them through the streets, paraded them around town, left them parked in the freezing cold where their bodies would not work, where their bodies failed them and all they could do was think, and all they could think was, *Get me out of here!*

And without really knowing it, Armand turned left on Blue Ridge Boulevard, then pulled onto Route 50 East toward Steingart's house.

The cat shifted in the box.

* * *

"Your wife here?" Armand asked him

"Of course not," Steingart said. "I told you she's at a conference."

"Was she at a conference when Lacy Johnson disappeared, three weeks ago Thursday?"

Steingart appeared to think about it. He wetted his thick lips. "She was visiting her mother, now that I think about it," he said.

"Yeah."

Steingart sipped his tea. He'd brought them both tea, though Armand hadn't asked for it.

"And when Wilma Perrin disappeared?"

"Now when was that again?" Steingart asked.

"December 7."

"Oh, dear. I don't remember where she was."

"She was out that evening," Armand said. "Parent-teacher conferences. I checked."

"Oh, yes," Steingart said. He sipped his tea again. "Is there a problem with that? She's not a suspect, is she?"

"No, it's just a funny coincidence." Armand drummed his uneasy fingers on the arm of the sofa, two taps with his ring finger, two with his pinky. It took some concentration. "Why are you smiling?" he asked at last. "Is this funny to you?"

"Of course not," Steingart said, still smiling.

"Is this a game? Is it some kind of game?"

"It's not a game."

Armand slid his hand into his jacket pocket, held his fist there to keep it from trembling, felt the cold steel of his service revolver. He'd taken it from the glove compartment of the Crown Vic before he knocked on Steingart's door. He looked long and deep into the other man's eyes. Steingart shifted modestly.

"Where's Elizabeth Wallace?"

"Who?"

"Elizabeth Wallace."

"Oh, dear," Steingart said.

"What did you do with her?"

"Oh, dear." He was still smiling.

Outside, snow decorated the windowsills. It came down and down over the rooftops and the parked cars. It fell big and luminous in the streetlights' glow. It fell big as aspirin tablets.

Armand withdrew the gun.

"She's in a tan Kia Sentra parked at the airport. Lot B, four or five spaces east of stop 7. She's probably still alive."

Jackson was silent on the other end of the phone. "What the fuck?" he said at last, but by then Armand had hung up.

It had been a pleasure getting the information out of Steingart. A real pleasure. And now he'd spent six hours driving in circles around the Plaza just thinking about it, watching the restaurants close, watching the bars close, watching as one by one the cars that lined the streets disappeared.

It was a beautiful snow. A lovely, numbing snow that decorated the windshield for just a moment before the wipers brushed it away. Again and again. For hours.

The cat meowed on the seat beside him. He still had to bring it to Lamar, but it was far too late now. Tomorrow. He'd do it tomorrow. Christmas Eve. It would be like a Christmas present.

And what did it matter if he retired six days before he'd intended? What did it matter if they put him in a box, in a cage? He was already in a cage and it got smaller every day.

The cat scratched at the box, stuck its paw through one of the air holes, meowed.

And the murderer in the trunk was just coming to—Armand could hear him back there moving, his first half-hearted kicks. Then the sound of the tire iron hitting the wheel wells, fists banging on the ceiling. "Let me out of here!" the murderer called.

Armand wondered if he ever would.

MISSION HILLS CONFIDENTIAL
BY GRACE SUH

Mission Hills

Allison sits in the breakfast room and watches the cardinal pair, male and female, dipping in and out of the holly bushes where they make their home. She avoids this room in the morning—too much sun. But it's tolerable starting from early afternoon, which it now is, when she can drink her tea and look out the tall windows and watch the shadows sit neatly under the trees like coasters.

Her husband Britt is upstairs in the green guest room. Since winter, when he fell in with a new group of friends, he's been tumbling into bed at all hours, reeking of vodka and smoke and sweat. A month ago she asked him to use a guest room on nights he goes out, and mostly he remembers. For some reason he eschews the gray one with the nautical theme and king-sized bed in favor of the mint-green one with the Colefax chinoiserie print that swathes the walls, draperies, armchair, and dainty canopy bed.

She doesn't know if he's alive. If he isn't dead, he's probably close. The last time she saw him was three hours ago, at ten in the morning. He was sprawled on the tall double bed, his great spread-eagled mass covering nearly the whole of it, bedclothes tangled around his legs. He was either OD'ing or unconscious, his hand cold, his breathing shallow, irregular pants. No visible pain or discomfort. No panic like last time. Pants and socks thrown on the floor. She felt for his phone in his pocket and hung the pants on the back of the bathroom door. Most likely the battery was dead, but just in case, this would make it that much harder for him.

The house is so vast, and the walls and floors so solid and

thick, that one can barely hear a thing from one room to the next. And the green guest room is over the library, clear on the other side of the house. In the house Allison grew up in, two blocks away, she and her father used the staticky intercom system to reach one another, but this house, though almost as large, is strangely without one.

Last time was two months ago. Allison awoke to screaming. It was six in the morning. A girl was shrieking so hysterically and insistently that the scream's gauzy overtones managed to travel up and penetrate her deep, early-morning sleep. Allison stumbled downstairs, slippers in hand, following the sound to the kitchen. A young woman and two men were standing over Britt, who lay sprawled on the floor between the island and the double ovens. Allison reached him and he began a kind of convulsion.

"Where's the shower?" the short guy yelled. "We got to get him in the shower!" As though the problem was that Britt was terribly dirty.

"Sit him up," said the other guy. He had that shaved head thing that bald guys do, and looked very tall, doubling over to get a closer look at Britt. "He's choking," he reported, unnecessarily. Britt was coughing in a retching, erupting way. The tall guy yanked him up and as he did Britt's eyes opened, the way a baby doll opens its eyes when tilted vertically. His eyeballs swung up and the lids closed again and then they opened and he looked stonily at his feet and said, "Unh uh uh."

Something about it struck Allison as comical. She almost laughed. Maybe she did. The girl had been kneeling on the floor next to Britt, her fat bare knees sprawled so that her short dress hiked up even shorter, her fat hands clutching her throat as she shrieked, "Do something! Do something!" But at the sight of Allison her face lit up. There was something avid about her, a squirrel's bright but distracted gaze shifting from emergency to stranger. She scrambled to her feet and lumbered forward, hand thrust out. "I'm Brandi! With an *i*!"

Britt mentioned these new friends sometimes, and weekend plans with them, with a child's disingenuous glee, but Allison didn't recall any mention of a girl. She'd figured the all-night techno and cocaine parties to be another of Britt's misguided temporary enthusiasms, like the brief but equipment-intensive saltwater fish tank winter and the car racing lessons and the filmmaking group.

Brandi was as chunky and plain as a Cabbage Patch Kid. She wore thick, emphatic makeup, massive high heels, and a dress so tight it bunched all around her. Her hips and thighs were enormous. She was young, maybe mid-twenties. What kind of people name a child after a liquor? "That's Nick," Brandi said, nodding at the tall man. "And Ilon."

Britt said, "Uh uh uh."

"Can you breathe?" Ilon asked.

They never had people over, so it was a shock to see strangers standing around. They'd been there who knows how long. Half-empty drinks littered the counter. Nick reached over and finished one off. There was a little pocket mirror at the far end, by the beverage sink, with a rolled-up bill beside it. That struck her as funny too. Like an '80s movie prop.

"That's a lot of granite," Brandi said, following Allison's eyes.

"Marble," Allison said. "Calacatta Oro."

"No," Britt gasped. "Can't breathe."

"Isn't granite better?" Brandi said. "Doesn't stain and stuff?"

Ilon pounded Britt on the back, like something had gone down the wrong way. "Britt!" he yelled, "Britt!" Or like Britt was suddenly deaf.

Ilon and Nick dragged him two rooms over to the library, Britt's bulk listing between the tall, bald man and the short, hairy man. They leaned him back on one of the red brocade sofas and everyone grouped around and watched him breathe. His skin looked white and damp as poached fish. He reached over with his right hand and walked his fingers over the dome of his torso to his heart. For a second it looked as though he was going to recite the Pledge of Allegiance. But instead he said, "My arm. Arm. Allison."

The three looked at her and Allison turned and ran upstairs. She put on clothes and running shoes and grabbed her purse and phone, and when she got back to the library Britt was staggering back and forth before the fireplace with his right hand still over his heart. "I'm dying," he said. "My heart won't stop."

"Okay," Allison said. "You should get in the car."

No one moved.

"I need help," she said.

Brandi went to the kitchen and returned with a giant purse made of shiny white leatherette. It was suddenly awkward, like a dinner party dispersing after an unforgivable scene. Ilon and Nick pushed Britt out the front door and into the back of Allison's car. Nick pulled the seat belt shoulder strap down but Britt shook his head violently no. His right hand was still stuck over his heart. "Nothing," he said.

Nick and Ilon got into the front of their car, parked behind Allison's Land Rover in the circular drive. Brandi stood with her hand on the Nissan's back door, watching Allison walk around. She gave her a little wave. "So is your dad the guy," she called in a conversational tone, "the one who died in jail?"

There was an hour wait before a triage nurse showed Britt down a corridor and up onto a gurney closely enclosed by polyester drapes. It was like being in a motel shower with two other people. Britt seemed revived by the imminence of medical care. He'd even made the walk from the waiting area by himself.

"What's the problem?" the nurse asked.

"Overdose," Britt said. Allison was surprised at his plain-speaking. "I had a heart attack or something from an overdose."

The nurse took his vitals. She inquired what substances he'd taken. Coke? Yes. How much. A lot. Two or three lines, repeated several times over the course of the night. Ecstasy? Two. Meth?

No. Heroin? No. Other opiates—Percocet, Percodan, Vicodin, OxyContin? One pill of something, at the beginning of the evening. Alcohol? Vodka tonics. Maybe five.

The nurse disappeared and no one came back for a long time. This must mean no dire danger. Britt seemed to think so too, because he cheered up. Flat on the gurney, he listened alertly to various commotions taking place around them. After a while he propped himself up on his elbows—a remarkably strenuous pose for one so hefty and so recently collapsed. He dug in his shorts pocket for his phone and took a glance. "No juice," he muttered. He turned to Allison with a bright smile. "Do you mind getting me something to drink? And some kind of snack? I need salt. Oh, and a magazine from the waiting room?"

Allison said nothing. She pointedly took her own phone out of her purse, having been reminded of its useful distractions, and resumed a game on the *New York Times* crossword app.

What she minded most was that stupid fat slut's invocation of her father. She didn't deserve to as much as speak of him. It wasn't just that this was the first time, in a very long time, a decade or more, that anyone had the stupidity and lack of tact to mention her father to her directly, it was also that the girl must have heard the story from Britt, meaning that he had betrayed her, wronged her, unforgivably.

"Do you hear me?" Britt said. He didn't notice that she hadn't yet said a word to him all morning. "Allison, water, I need water."

"You could have died," Allison said at last. "Next time, you will."

"I know, yes," Britt said. He thinks she is nagging—not predicting, not telling him. "I'll be more careful."

He won't, she thought. It's only a matter of time, probably days, before he's back to the usual. Whatever Britt is, he's not moderate. He drinks a lot. Smokes a lot. His favorite foods are Town Topic cheeseburgers and onion rings, his second favorite giant platters of pasta piled with meat sauce and melted cheese at

Garozzo's or Carmen's. Some mornings he goes and gets an entire flat box of Lamar's: apple fritters and cinnamon cake donuts and frosted Long Johns filled with whipped cream that has the pearlescent sheen and delightfully slick, frothy mouthfeel of nondairy, highly artificial ingredients. His own dad died of a massive coronary at age fifty-one, Britt's age now.

At the emergency room, he was told to return for follow-up EKGs and to make an appointment with a cardiologist, but he never did. No matter what she does or doesn't do today, the amount she's shortening his life is probably not appreciable.

Even now, fifteen years after his death, people talk about her dad—nasty, hypocritical things. To hear them, you'd think this fair town was a stranger to financial malfeasance, rather than a regular hornets' nest of it. She could drive up and down the pleasant lanes of the neighborhood and point out mansion after lovely mansion bought and paid for with embezzlement, blackmail, exploitation, and every other kind of scoundrel behavior and white-collar criminal activity, felony-class and otherwise. Certainly her father wasn't the first nor the last from this town to be sent to the minimum security facility in Minnesota.

The talk is idly malign, the chatter of strangers, not directed at her. *They just bought a house on that block, you know, the Mission Hills Swindler Street.* Or *Bold as Gould.* Stuff like that. Local color.

To Allison, Morris Gould was a good father, a good parent. The only one she had, really. Her mother was sick from as early as Allison could remember, had been her entire adult life. Hence Allison's adoption.

Mostly what Allison remembers is her mother leaning listless at the breakfast table after chemo, lips cracked, or sitting motionless in a wicker chaise in the solarium, wrapped in a quilted satin robe—the robe vermillion, the chaise cobalt, its cushions a riot of chintz, the scarf on her head brilliantly printed, her small face beneath, colorless.

She died two days before Allison's tenth birthday, and then it was Allison and her father in the big Tudor pile on Verona. Consuelo came Monday through Friday, seven in the morning to butter Allison's toast. Her father drove her to school, a terrycloth Chiefs robe over his pajamas, shearling slipper mocs on his bare feet, window cracked an inch even in freezing weather as a purely symbolic, wholly ineffectual nod to the smoke billowing from his Pall Mall. If anything, the slipstream pushed the smoke to the passenger side, rather than allowing it to waft over his head. He didn't generally commence conversation until sometime around lunch, but as he pulled up to Sunset Hill, he'd throw her a winking, cigarette-clenched smile and pat her shoulder as she slid out of the beat-up Jaguar.

He was there again in the afternoon, one of the few fathers in the line of pickup parents. Even in winter he'd be outside, leaning against the car, Soviet spy-chic in ushanka and sunglasses, puffing on a cigarette, hands plunged deep into the pockets of his Mongolian-wool overcoat. Sometimes underneath he'd still be in his pajamas and Chiefs robe.

Consuelo waited until Allison got home so she could give her a kiss on the hairline before she left for the day. She referred to her as *pobrecita* and did what she could to assuage the sorrow and void she imagined was life without a mother, mostly by starching her clothes so stiffly they could barely be pulled off the hangers, and cooking and baking enough for lumberjacks. The house was so big she had enough to do just rotating through the unused rooms, vacuuming and waxing floors and dusting banisters and shining the leaves on the plants in the solarium and rolling up rugs and sending them out to be cleaned. No one ever went up to the third floor, once a ballroom, which was dimly lit and piled with old furniture and boxes of papers and books, nor to the moldering stone-walled basement, a tangle of ancient bicycles and sports equipment from her father's youth, metal parts rusted and leather straps cracked.

Her mother's dry cleaner–bagged clothing stayed hanging

in her closet, tissue-stuffed handbags and wooden-treed shoes and tissue-wrapped cardigans stacked by color remaining on the shelves. In the drawers of the peach dressing room, her lipsticks were lined up by tube length. In the endless silence of the afternoons Allison sometimes sat in the gold scroll-work vanity chair and stroked waxy lipsticks on her lips, but her mother had been blond, with a pink complexion and neat mouth, a Pat Nixon type. On Allison's olive skin, round Asian face, and full lips, the frosty pinks and gold-sparkled corals looked garish and improbable.

What her father did all day was harder to answer. Enormous, heavy, cut-glass ashtrays the size of candy bowls in hues of topaz and amber were set all around the house, dozens of them. The ones most often filled and even overflowing with half-smoked butts, as though the by-product of great industry, occupied the corner of the giant leather-topped desk in the dark library downstairs, and the center of the white Parsons cube between the boxy microsuede Italian lounge chairs in the study off his bedroom upstairs. What was he doing while all this smoking took place? *Managing accounts*, that was the only phrase she ever heard. Stacks of manila folders spilled next to ashtrays. And everywhere there were telephones—the heavy, old-fashioned kind with long, tangled cords—well into the 1980s. He smoked and talked on those phones.

Morris Gould was born in that house. His father, Harmon, had it built himself in the late 1940s, from the proceeds of a fur and real estate business that disappeared sometime in the interim. When they drove around downtown her father might gesture toward an empty and abandoned department store or pharmacy building with his cigarette and say, "Dad owned that one," or, "He sold that one in the '60s, when all this was empty. Made almost nothing."

The family were suspect in Mission Hills from the start—Jews. So what, screw them. Harmon got around the Jew-excluding covenants by paying a third party to buy the land and build the house as if for himself. Like all Jews they were barred from the club down the road—her dad called it the KKKC Country Club. When he was young his parents were members at Oakwood, but by the time she came along he'd dropped the membership. Too far from home.

There were lots of Jews in Mission Hills by then, at Sunset Hill too. Not that she was considered one, being plainly not. At school she was friends mostly with Priya, a girl only three years removed from Delhi, whose parents were residents at the university hospital. It was a friendship she never thought to carry off the grounds. After school the other girls gaggled off in twos and threes and fours, to slumber parties and birthday parties and swim meets. The world of tennis skirts and tartan headbands and sunshine was not for her. She looked forward every day to returning to the murky depths and heavy, unbestirred air of their house. Loved the dense, voluminous falls of velvet drapery that rippled over the casement windows and pooled on the floor and could barely be pushed aside, loved the dark ornamental woodwork and paneling, the soothing silence and room after room empty of people.

On weekends, when it was only the two of them, it was enough just to sit for hours in solitude, exquisitely aware of all that uninhabited, enveloping space, feeling in perfect company, knowing that her father sat, also in solitude, also in great peace, down a long hallway, or downstairs. The metric tons of buffering brick and stone, plateaus of marble, the scant two acres of groomed, densely planted grounds, too steeply sloped to be usable for outdoor recreation—everything about the house suited them perfectly.

Which is to say that she understood, perfectly, why her father did what they say he did, what he was convicted of doing, what they put him in jail for. Why it was necessary. How could they live any other way? How could the house not be theirs? He did it for her. The censure of the public didn't bother her, their easy judgment, their shunning. She has never cared what they thought. They don't understand anything, not what is important.

The assets were dissolved while her father was in prison, so he didn't have to see the house put on the market, and the horrific estate sale with the invasion of slovenly bargain hunters, swarming like sweatpanted ants, grasping boxes of silverware and resting Royal Derby tureens on their beer guts. It was her senior year at KU. She skipped classes and drove over from Lawrence to watch. What was worse, that hundreds grubbed through her mother's pristine Jaeger and St. John's wool jersey and bouclé suits? Or that in the end most of her mother's clothing—bought in the smallest size and tailored even tinier around her narrow bird waist—went unsold and was dumped at the thrift store?

The house was sold to a guy who flipped it two years later at a huge profit, and for nearly a year construction trucks trundled in and out of the driveway. They said the entire interior was nearly gutted and reconstructed, the main floor "opened up, for casual entertaining." Desecration. Paradise renovated. Even the lawn was terraced, many of the trees taken down. More opening up.

Her father's sentence was five years, reduced to three for good behavior and because, in the second year, the cancer was discovered. Brandi should have listened to Britt's story more carefully, because what Morris Gould did not do was die in jail. He received the first course of treatment in the prison clinic, but they let him out for what turned out to be his last four months. It was almost better when he was in prison. At least there his medical care was paid for, his meals provided. He had no insurance by that time, and everything had to be paid out of pocket. There was a trust from Allison's grandfather, who'd generously and promptly set it up at her adoption at age twenty months, fortunately so, since he died shortly after. And another trust created by her father that was also left intact. From these she bought the medications and paid the hospital bills, and then the funeral bills, and at the end was left with enough to afford a condo in downtown Chicago, where she had found a job as a cog in a Big Eight accounting firm—quite a delicious irony for the daughter of a white-collar felon. This is the glory of America, where the crimes of the father are not visited upon his child. Except in gossip, of course. That is a life sentence.

The ironic job was soon after resigned, the Wrigleyville condo unbought; for Priya, by then a dermatology fellow in Phoenix, had flown in for the funeral, and when they were out to dinner together the next evening to catch up, they ran into Britt Fuller, whom Priya knew slightly from KU Med. Britt had graduated from medical school with Priya, but dropped out of residency the next year. He'd been a nontraditional student anyway, having entered on a lark at age thirty-five after a young adulthood of rich-boy bumming. The way he put it, the car repair part of medicine wasn't interesting enough for the twenty-four-hour shifts. Not worth staying up for, he joked.

Britt was also an only child, also an orphan, of a family whose three-generations-old firm manufactured road resurfacing machinery. Britt was a year out of Rockhurst when his father had the heart attack. His mother died two months later, in an outbreak of Legionnaire's disease on the Caribbean cruise she was taking as relief from her bereavement. Britt has nothing to do with the company, but because of the family's controlling share (a paternal uncle, who lives in Seattle and practices craniosacral healing, is the only other beneficiary), he has no need to seek employment.

Allison knew he was rich right away, before she learned any of this. No obvious markers. No watch. So-so wallet. His physical appearance was that of a corrupt old-timey banker, with his thick, prematurely silver hair, solid girth, and square, not unhandsome head, but he dressed like a character out of *The Matrix*, in black leather pants, a long black leather coat, and pointy black boots with too much heel, acres of leather on his ample frame. At the very least, it was an unusual look for a Plaza restaurant on a Thursday night. Chatting with Priya, he grabbed their bill folder from the waitress and stuffed in a stack of cash, way more than enough, without so much as glancing at the total. An obnoxious thing to do. Priya raised an eyebrow, but Allison didn't mind. Her father might have done the same. Already she was taken by Britt's air of complete indifference, the prick demeanor of one beholden to no one. It's something that can't be cultivated or pretended. It means money. Piles and piles. Lettuce. Lucre. Spondulicks, as her father used to say.

Britt was forty-one. She was twenty-six. A not indecent age spread. He should have been one of the most eligible bachelors in KC. Never married. Independent fortune—not as many of those in town as you'd think. And he was not quite fat yet, although he was getting there fast. But there was something off about him, and no one wanted him. Maybe it was the schizophrenic wardrobe, shifting from one ridiculous costume to the next: the black leather thing and a punk look with tight red pants and combat boots and a strange gaucho thing, with pleated shirts and embroidered vests and hats. There was barely a normal item in his closet. It was as though he deliberately chose clothing that highlighted his ever-increasing plumpness and inner instability.

She didn't mind. Any of it. Not the way he leaked involuntary noises—little unprotected moans and sighs, like an infant fitfully sleeping—as though in private moments he immediately reverted to attending to long-nourished inner complaints and slights. Not the way his hand felt grabbing her breast—heavy and possessive but also oddly careless, a general undirected pawing. This led to rapid, panicked humping, and when he came, he yelled, and collapsed on her with huge heaving gasps and wrapped his giant self around her neat body.

Everything about her was smooth and sleek. Her small pretty hands with their shiny polished nails. Her smooth, surprisingly solid legs, free of hair and ripples and veins. Her smooth concave belly that never grew. They used no birth protection but nothing ever happened. That was fine. Britt never mentioned children. And she had never wanted so much as a pet. She had what she wanted. They lived in the house Britt grew up in, only a street away from her old house. It was also a Tudor, laid out almost the same. She changed nothing in it, except to put up blinds in the south-facing windows.

You could say she married Britt for his money, but that wouldn't be exactly true. She married him for a security for which money was necessary but not sufficient, for a solid feeling of returning to what was rightfully hers. To live any other way would have felt like fraud, and the oddness of him, his lack of friends, the way he was set at an angle to the rest of the world—that was something to return to also. Besides, she felt always profound gratitude for how little he cared, when he learned who her father was. Being morally off himself, he didn't judge.

There was, at the core of their strange union, a unity. Once, when he and a filmmaking buddy drove past the old Gould house, now with so many trees removed, more visible to the street than before, and spreading impressively high and wide on the rise, the buddy gestured at it with his thumb: "Guy who used to own that chiseled millions, story made the *Wall Street Journal*." Not realizing that he was speaking to the son-in-law of the late villain himself. When Britt reported this to Allison, there was a certain surge in his voice, a jocularity he could not tamp, not all the way, that spoke of a joy he should not have felt. All the same, the fact that he told her suggested a kind of loyalty, a loyalty she cherished more than love.

But the loyalty is gone. Now there is nothing. She knew it the second Brandi asked her that question. She knew even before that, the minute she saw Brandi, and the way Brandi's eyes assessed her in such a proprietary way, a rival sizing up the competition.

Allison's tea is cold. She is still in her workout clothes and running shoes. She took her four-mile walk up and down the hills this morning, same as she does every morning. The usual joggers and mothers pushing three-wheeled strollers saw her and waved. There are fewer exercisers out on weekends than during the week, but still, enough of the regulars saw her to testify if there are police inquiries. She doubts there will be, anyway. This isn't *Law & Order*. This is Mission Hills. With the emergency room visit two months ago, and Britt's physical condition and family medical history, no one will question the obvious scenario.

Allison assumes Britt and Brandi have had sex. Or tried. She's read that coke renders the dick nonfunctional. As for Allison and Britt, not a thing has happened in a long time. Before that, things had dried up to once every several months or so—after all, they'd been married ten years—but he hasn't made a move toward her in ages.

The question is: would Britt leave Allison, his wife of a decade, for a heavily padded, lightly educated fat girl from Raytown, or wherever she's from? It's hard to imagine. He has a class thing as much as Allison does. There are reasons why Britt was a forty-one-year-old bachelor when they met. He is passive and lacking initiative. He favors routine, dislikes change. Still, she can't take the chance. Not when that girl would snatch him up in a second.

The hands of the sunburst clock on the wall hitch at every five-minute mark. The lilac-print wallpaper behind the breakfront is faded from decades of eastern sun, but that is part of its charm. She doesn't understand her neighbors' constant need to renovate and redecorate. She chalks it up to boredom. She and Britt never have guests; no one sees the wallpaper. Even if they did, what does it matter what people think?

She will wait one more hour. At two o'clock she will walk upstairs and into the mint-green guest room. She doesn't think it likely that he'll be alive. Whatever she finds, she will dial 911. They will take him away. As for her, she will never be moved from this house.

COME MURDER ME NEXT, BABE

BY DANIEL WOODRELL

12th Street

S haron's husband died from boredom—hers, not his. He was a nightshift drone in Raytown who liked the drudgery, wanted only a plain life with his wife and daughter in a box house, slipping toward eternity, neither blamed nor noticed. He slept on the couch most days. The way his mouth jumped open and honked when he slept made her sadness swell—so left out of the pretty world, the world denied her—his lips reminding her of the leavings she scraped off plates into the garbage pail four lunch shifts a week at Catfish Billy's. She watched her husband, sleeping or awake, eyes fixed on his slack, lumpish lips and receding chin, and thought, *The fucking leavings have followed me home and joined his face. I feel bugs with his smell running loose in my veins!*

She was eighteen, said she was twenty, and had every appetite, none of which he could satisfy.

Sharon loved Thunderbirds, and she loved them in any color so long as it was blue. She'd slip her panties free under her skirt and toss them out the window of a speeding Thunderbird and discreetly bang a guy in the parking lot at Winstead's just for giving her a ride and a chance to feel quickly alive before the duller world found her again and smothered her joy. Cruise down Main and circle the Plaza, in a set of wheels that roared through her dreams, the city lights so bright and whispering excitedly that all she craved existed, it was all here, right behind the golden doors of Jasper's or the Savoy Grill, places where the people who mattered chewed with their mouths closed and their cufflinks gleaming. She'd cruise happily with the stranger of the day, excited by the fintails, the soft white seats plush against her bare ass, and she'd smile, smile and sigh. She craved Thunderbirds like her mother craved Jesus, but she craved them harder and knew where to find them.

She called all her boyfriends Bub, to keep them straight.

One sunny morning in that crackerbox house she spread her arms in the living room and when she found she could span her reach to both walls at once, she went into the bedroom for the pistol in the bottom bureau drawer. He slept on the couch, a miserable figure, far too plain in every detail, honking that honk, the leavings huffing in and out, and she put the pistol into the tiny mitts of the two-year-old whose arrival had doomed her, leaned the barrel to the sleeping head, let the goddamn kid take the rap. Hubby died before he could blink. The toddler bawled and hid under the coffee table. Sharon said, "Bless your heart, hon, don't cry—it was an accident."

One cop smelled her untamed scent and felt creeped-out by her strange affability; he told the chief that no toddler that small would be strong enough to jerk the trigger on a revolver, but he was ignored. It went down as a tragedy of an innocent nature and Sharon danced alone all night in the backyard singing to the only audience that mattered.

I fell in love with her through the pages of the *Kansas City Star*. A fifteen-year-old on 72nd Street in desperate need of mutual lubrication and associations that would bring a sinister edge to consciousness—she found me with her lupine eyes, beckoning from the front page, above the fold. *Why not grow some guts, you sissy, and come run with me as long as you last?* She was so much who she was, always, in any circumstance, that her looks didn't matter, though she had those too. The bouffant of that year, the prim dresses and little Easter hats on a smokey-eyed killer, admitted her into my fantasies where she took root and ruled; and after the first mistrial I rode the bus downtown and wandered expectantly, as though she might be cruising 12th Street in that perfectly blue

Thunderbird the insurance bought, looking for a male to seduce and fuck silly and snuff to feel that tingle once more. I went down-town often to volunteer my dick for her needs, my throat to her knife. I stood outside the corner drugstore where the burlesque girls rushed from the back doors of the Pink Pussy Cat and the Folies de Paris to buy makeup and barbiturates and greasepaint. I stood among the erotic artists smelling of sex and the damp wicked world and waited to be found by Sharon. Whatever beautiful evil she did would be oh, so worth it, if she did it to me—gun, knife, strangling cord from a lamp. I puffed with hope for an electric-black finish and kissed the *Star* every time she went on trial again.

The early trials were not about the dead husband, that came later. There were many obstacles in Sharon's life, individuals who stymied her dreams, and she tended to murder them, promptly. (If she saw something she wanted she was instinctive as a wolf—if she could catch it, she ate it, and you don't call wolves evil for their hunger; you see their powerful, pretty, and pitiless eyes, the mortal elegance of their moves, admire their elemental cunning, even, and when the wolf was Sharon you wanted sex too, in the weeds, under the stars—tear those pantyhose wide, spread that skirt, get lost feeding among the wild hunting thighs and ruffed fur.) Her crimes were so little planned yet boldly executed that she was very difficult to convict, as pure brio carried the day, most days, but the law is a relentless pest to the wild among us and keeps on coming with those cuffs and chains.

She liked blended scotch, plenty of rocks, things that glittered with apparent value, fake or real, and more, more of everything that appealed, everything that brought water to her mouth, ev-erything that might satisfy her bottomless want for even a day, an hour, the length of time it took new silken unmentionables to fall from her body.

Thunderbirds again. His name was Roger, a married man with kids; he sold Thunderbirds, spent his days surrounded by a glory of them, in all colors and a few vintages, and she liked him for his

Thunderbirds, and he liked the sudden, scorching sex. He grew fond of her hot habit of bouncing with all her sizzle squeezing on his dick till it felt like it might melt soft and be smeared away with the very next bounce. But he miscalculated his fuck-buddy horribly, kept his naked time with her brief, too brief, their meetings were limited, too limited, the wife, blame the wife, the kids and that goddamn wife, always some sort of shadow looming between Sharon and that big shiny feeling she chased everywhere.

I wanted to mail her a key to our front door, with directions to our house and a promise to die in the basement rumpus room however she wanted, make it special, astonish me, garnish your altar with my remains, but couldn't find an address of any sort. Love asks so much of us when we are young and everything when we are old.

Roger's wife answered her knocks and Sharon must have felt a sinking sensation; the wife was gorgeous. No wonder he was so slippery.

The gorgeous wife said, "Yes?"

"I have the saddest news, Mrs. G—my sister is cheating with a married man, and he's your husband."

"I don't believe it."

"They're parked in a field a couple of miles from here. I feel so awful, that it's my sister doing this, and they do it all the time, I'm ashamed to say, but she just won't listen to me. I'll take you to them so you can see for yourself and stop things from getting worse—you have a family to defend."

The prosecutor waited several months to file charges because they couldn't find the murder weapon; they finally went to trial without it. Many pictures of her in the *Star*, looking unconcerned and stylish, making me state aloud my sacred vows to that dangerous tilted chin and flameless eyes, until the headline appeared: *MISTRIAL!*

She became a criminal celebrity with qualities they admired on 12th Street. The broken-nosed guys and whorish gals took her under their wings. She posted bond for the retrial, then posted bond again when charged with hubby's murder. She could be found stalking under the neon lights that gave 12th Street and her life the dramatic tinge she sought and adored— smoking, laughing, swinging on the arms of starstruck gangsters and smitten cops, eating the finest beef in Kansas City while sitting at Harry Truman's favorite table, hitting mom-and-pop pasta joints in Northeast or rib joints on Brooklyn and Armour, Sanderson's Lunch at three a.m. for a greaseburger to soak up the scotch, waking wherever she fell, pulling on yesterday's salty dress before wobbling to the sidewalk and crooking her finger at the next Bub she saw.

I, too, wandered beneath those lights of many colors, in continental slacks, Beatle boots, and a paisley shirt, stood on the corner waiting and knew this: it would do no good to be polite to her on 12th Street, gentlemanly. She would snicker at polite. Polite or gentlemanly behavior would make her snicker, and then she'd yank your wallet from your pocket and take all the folding money, throw down a couple of your own dollars before you, and say, "Have a bottle of pop on me, candy ass, then beat it." You wouldn't want her to snicker and rob you in public like that, it makes you feel so very small, and too alert to your own smallness, so you'd best come on to her a little bit rough, or a lot rough, show her some edges, smile wide and rich and snarly. Then, she'd be more fun than you've ever had. If Sharon just once took you into her embrace for a night, or most of a night, you'd leave rearranged and poor but made fresh again by the natural world and what it can do when it likes you and feels like fucking.

Who wouldn't love her?

She made the courts and law and juries look like suckers at her command. Mistrial, mistrial, and a new trial announced, then the murder weapon was discovered behind her mother's stove by new residents; and she said to her current Bub, a bartender at the Pussycat named Tony, of course: "I am magic, but I can't be magic every day—better roll toward Mexico. Coming?"

In Mexico City: Did Raul Sedillo Ortiz have a gold tooth that beckoned? A watch with diamond inlays that glittered until you felt a fever? Did the rude weasel ask you to pay for the drinks like you weren't a lady? Tony fled north toward home, glad to get away whole, and all alone you went to the Casa Verde with your first Mexican Bub and . . . did he call you *puta* while you blew him?

Convicted in Mexico, then disappeared from prison at Christmas of 1970, and there's never been another photo of her above the fold for me to view and cherish. Killed by guards? Did the family of the dead man pay for her escape so they could execute her as they saw fit? Or did she make it to Honduras where by coincidence her lawyer owned seventeen thousand acres? That's plenty of jungle.

I feel her yet alive and no longer in Honduras. I feel her relocated to a brownstone overlooking Brush Creek, laughing to herself every morning as she exercises in Loose Park, a spry lady with a reshaped face and a loping gait. I feel . . . a wish, an old, lost wish, that she'd seen me once on the corner with my neck bared and my soul craving, understood me at a glance, had me for a snack, let me sleep hugging the pillow with her stink in the threads, then dispatched me about four a.m.; at the peak of my life, the existential summit, removed me from the herd, snuffed perfectly, before the horror unfolds. The fifty years of trudging bored flat toward an eternity of the dull; deader while standing than her victims laying underground, never feeling a timeless blade or seeing the goodbye flash from a barrel; never so alive as that one night you didn't have when the wolf had at you in the old Muehlebach and murder was in the air with desire and despair and every vessel pumped inside your chest until you and the wild came together at that spot where the pale and dark worlds kiss and love is in the deed if not the word.

THE SOFTEST CRIME

BY MATTHEW ECK

41st and Walnut

for James Crumley

I first met Alice four years ago in Kansas City at a conference for people affected by violent crimes. She was the daughter of a serial killer who had murdered forty-five women on the West Coast, and I was the son of a serial killer who had murdered fourteen people on the East Coast. We'd only gone to the conference because we'd both recently moved to Kansas City to get away from those who associated our names with the criminal way. It was our first and last attempt at one of those gatherings. There were more people there than you would imagine.

We met at the bar in the lobby of the Hyatt on the last day of the conference and then spent the next two weeks in and out of each other's beds. But we were a wreck together, and knew it. Our grief followed us kiss to kiss and bed to bed, so we agreed at last to leave each other alone.

Then last year, the day after her father died, she called me and asked if I wanted to meet for drinks at The Cashew. She said there was a movie she wanted to see that was showing tomorrow at the art house near 20th and Grand. She asked if I'd like to see it with her before we went out for drinks. I said I would.

The last big storm of the year moved through the city the night before we met. Two feet of snow fell in three hours. I watched it from the window of my apartment. I'd wanted to see her in all those intervening years that fell between our first parting. I watched the snowfall and tried to caress my emotions with a twelve-pack of beer. There was a point in the night where the electricity went out for about an hour. I lived in an apartment building at the corner of 41st and Walnut. From my window I could see that the lights were still on over the Plaza and north toward Midtown.

I laced up a pair of my old army boots and went out front with a can of beer so that I could measure the snow for myself with a good walk. I peered up into the falling snow and imagined myself an animal in the wild. A buck, a horse, a pig, a fox. I wanted to see the stars. I wanted to feel placed in my heart. But I couldn't see them because there was still too much light in the other parts of the city.

I threw the beer can toward the door of the apartment building and walked toward the Art Institute. It felt good to walk in the snow with my breath blooming in front of me. The campus was dark from the outage. I had wanted to see the lights that usually guided someone across campus. School was out for the winter, so it was quiet. I crossed to the Nelson-Atkins Museum of Art and stood in the middle of the large lawn. A few cars hummed past in the street. Mine were the first prints in the snow.

"Where now?" I whispered to the sky. I took a step and turned myself in a circle, forcing a smile. "Who now?"

There are days we must feel as far from ourselves as the ocean feels from the moon.

Let me admit it here, I missed her when she was not around. Yes, we had parted ways, but we had never resolved anything. She said as much. Two weeks together had left us shattered against the rocks of the other. But I wanted more shattering. I wanted a year of her. I wanted a year and a day, at least.

Let me admit this as well, Alice was never her real name.

Boys, note this well: women make poor receptacles for your dreams.

Girls, note this well: men make poor receptacles for your dreams.

We are not chalices to be filled with hope.

Yet I long for someone to prove me wrong.

* * *

Her father killed forty-five women in ten years across the Pacific Northwest. My father murdered fourteen women across eight years in upstate New York and into Canada. The towns had names and so did the victims, but I will leave them out in this account, because so far as I know there are no ghosts haunting those towns. So let them sleep where they may, those ghosts.

I joined the army shortly after my father's arrest. Part of me wanted to get away from the media. Another part simply wanted to see the world. It was only later that I recognized what I really wanted was a sense of atonement for crimes I never committed. I moved to Kansas City after spending a few years watching the dirty work of empire up close in Iraq and Afghanistan. I was in and out of a marriage almost immediately. Then I read the article in the paper about the convention and so I went, and so I met her.

She was smart and shy, beautiful, of course. And then a week passed and everything that had felt right about our being together started to feel wrong. Once again, we were owned by our guilt for reasons we couldn't explain.

There was a documentary on about her father the other day. It's always returning to us, the past.

I drove through the empty, snow-covered streets of downtown to the art house cinema near 20th and Grand. I'd worked at that cinema the summer I moved to the city. I think she knew this and it must have been why she invited me to go with her.

I'd always liked working at the art house for the owner, Patrick. The theater sold PBR by the can for a dollar and Patrick didn't mind those days we drank a few through our shifts. The theater also had a nice old wooden bar off the balcony where Patrick and I used to sip scotch with our PBR while we listened to the sound of the movie coming through the curtains. I left the job when the fall semester started at UMKC.

She'd invited me to see *Breathless*. I had seen it before, but couldn't remember it other than the gesture of his thumb rubbing his lips. I couldn't remember whether love was celebrated or destroyed in the film. Or whether love was some vacant cause.

Patrick smiled when he saw me. He opened a can of PBR and handed it to me. I took a sip and leaned against the counter.

I turned when the door opened and it was Alice, her eyes bright and her smile wide for me. We hugged and held each other for a long time. Her breath felt like heaven against my neck.

"You look great," I said, leaning toward her.

"You too," she said, her eyes closed.

I could feel a few strands of her hair stick in the stubble on my chin as I pulled away from her.

I bought our tickets and Patrick handed her a can of beer. Her gloves were on so I took the can and opened it for her. I introduced the two of them.

"The beer's on the house," Patrick said. "You're the only two here, so drink up. We're still waiting on the film. It's on its way up from Wichita. They were showing it there last night, and I'm guessing the roads between here and there are slowgoing. They got a lot more snow than us."

I looked out the front door and saw mounds of snow rising onto the edge of the sidewalk, spilling over into the gutter. It was the typical dirty snow of any city sidewalk.

"They called a few hours ago," he said, "so they should be close. You can go ahead and sit down. I'll bring you a few more beers if it looks like it's going to be awhile."

We walked into the theater and sat in the middle of a row near the back. We looked at each other for a few minutes and just smiled. She touched my cheek with a gloved hand and I closed my eyes. I opened them when she took her hand away.

"I'm moving tomorrow," she said.

"Why?" I asked.

"I changed my name. I'm tired of people asking me if I'm related to the Moon River Killer."

Her last name was distinct enough that people must have asked her all the time. Her father had been one of the most notorious serial killers in history. There were days when I had thought of changing my name, but I knew it could take me only so far away from the truth.

She put the beer in the little cup holder and took her gloves off. She folded them and tucked them into the pocket of her coat. The skin around her thumbnail was cracked so that a little speck of bright pink flesh showed.

"I love these old movies." She curled a bit of hair around her finger and then chewed on it for a moment before tucking it behind her ear. "They're always about knights in shining armor and dirty blondes."

I nodded quietly at the screen and tried to see my face up there, the grin of the hero on my lips.

She started twisting another bit of hair to put behind the other ear. "I cried myself to sleep last night. I wish I could say it was the first time this year. How about you—when was the last time you cried yourself to sleep?"

I shook my head not knowing. "Last night?" I offered. "Would that be the right answer?"

She put a hand on my arm and said, "Yes." She looked at me, her blue eyes wet with sorrow. "Yes," she said, again. "Yes."

I liked her hand on my arm. She gently rubbed it before taking hold of my hand.

We sat in the soft light of the theater waiting for the lights to go all the way down and for the old cartoon that signaled the start of the film was near. I wondered what it meant to move at this time of the year, to drive through the hard dark of a winter night toward a new home. I wondered what it was like to go by a new name, the old one left alone to gather dust on some shelf in the basement.

I could have used a new name. I could have used a new city to haunt, with new troubles and new pleasures to tremble my lips.

Let us all drive through the dark toward a new home, the heart of winter shaking the air around us like a bell rung deep.

"I wish we shared better secrets," I said.

"Like how to measure love?" she asked.

"Like how to measure love."

"Instead of by days and weeks and years," she said, holding my hand tight.

"Like two weeks."

"Like two weeks," she said. "We did have fun though."

"We were okay."

"Don't undo it yet," she said. "Not while I'm still here."

She gently squeezed my hand and I did the same to hers. We turned our faces and stared at the different walls for a moment.

"What's your new name?" I asked.

"I can't tell you," she said. "It'll make it easier if you don't know."

I shifted in my seat and my shoes briefly stuck to the floor. I looked up at the screen. I looked at the walls. I looked at my hands. I didn't know where to look because I knew she was watching me. I stretched my hands, open, closed.

"Easier for me," I said softly.

"Both of us," she said.

I knew that I should have agreed, but part of me always felt that no matter how hard we were on our emotions, the pain of our loss was worth the price of our pleasure.

"Where are you moving?" I asked. "Can you tell me that?"

She shook her head no.

"Easier," I said.

She nodded.

She leaned toward me and kissed me gently on the lips.

"You should buy me some popcorn," she said.

"Would you like some popcorn?" I asked.

"It's like you read my mind."

I brought the bucket of popcorn back. She'd taken her coat

off and the warmth and perfumed smell of her body made my head hum. We ate the popcorn and were quiet for a few minutes.

"I like to take the popcorn home with me," she said. "Did you know that?"

"I did."

"I never eat it all, but I always buy the biggest one. You made the right choice on that." She tapped the side of the container.

"I didn't want to look cheap," I said.

She smiled and took another handful and ate it. "People think it's weird when they see you leaving the theater with a bucket of popcorn. They think it's like the furniture, something you should leave behind. My dates must think I'm crazy. I'll take it with me when we go and I'll leave it in their car or carry it out to drinks with us. Then at the end of the night, after we kiss, I carry it upstairs with me and leave them behind."

We were quiet. It was like the silence inside a bell. I touched my thumb to my lips. I touched my thumb to hers.

"You cannot touch silence," I said.

She smiled and touched her thumb to my lips. We ate more popcorn.

"It always bothered me that my father killed someone with the same name as me," she said. She chewed softly. "I could never fuck a man who has his name." She turned to me. "Would you ever fuck someone with your mother's name?"

"I don't know," I said. "No one with that name has ever asked."

She liked this and laughed loudly.

"How many times have you seen this film?" I asked.

"Once. But you can hold my hand if you get scared." She smiled at the screen. "Or you can just hold my hand. I don't mind right now. I don't know why but I feel warm for the first time in weeks."

I wanted to ask her what she was thinking about. I always wanted to ask her.

"We always made the sheets sing," she said.

"Then why didn't it work?"

"Because we were hell on each other's emotions. You know that."

"Yes," I said, and I did see it. But I had always hoped that we could work past this.

"We're owned by guilt," she said.

"Are you packed?" I asked.

"Mostly."

The owner came in and told us that it would be another hour. "Let me buy you a real drink," he said.

We walked up to the balcony and sat at a table that overlooked the lobby. She hugged the popcorn to her chest. She put the popcorn on the table and glanced around the room. She bit at her lips and rubbed my hand.

Patrick came back with a Jameson and a Guinness for each of us. He raised the Jameson and we toasted the weather.

"Are you originally from here?" she asked Patrick.

"No," he said. "St. Louis."

"Everyone is from somewhere else these days," she said, staring off into the distance.

"That is true," Patrick agreed. He smiled at me and walked back downstairs to the lobby.

"We own the town we come from in our heart," she said. "But we don't own people, we own problems."

Outside the snow swirled in the street. The Jameson went down easy in the fading light of the bar. I wondered what the first name she ever whispered was. I wondered what would be the last.

When the movie arrived we went back to the theater. We were still the only two there. The weather had kept everyone away. The lights finally fell and the projector illuminated the darkness. Dust particles sparkled in the projector's swath of light.

She leaned toward me and we kissed. We took the kiss far before we parted.

"You can be my knight in shining armor," she said.

"You can be my dirty blonde," I said.

She smiled and parted my lips with another kiss.

"When was your last good kiss?" she asked.

I watched her eyes move gently back and forth between my eyes. I didn't want to answer.

"We shouldn't have met when I was so lonely," she said.

"You're not lonely anymore?" I asked.

"No, I've gone further than loneliness allows."

I studied her face against the light of the film. She ate a little more popcorn. She turned and stared at me. We kissed again. Her lips were salty with the taste of popcorn, her breath warm from the Jameson.

"We should watch some of the movie," she said.

I agreed.

I watched the film and thought about how none of the fairy tales I knew had prepared me for my life. I thought about all those myths we'd studied in school, how none of them had held together in the end, and how they were as fragile as the truth.

We left our cars at the theater and walked through the snow toward The Cashew. But when we got there she said there was another bar, a kind of speakeasy, around the corner that she'd heard about. She kept insisting it was one more turn away. We rounded several corners and never found it. We hailed the one taxi we saw and took it back to her apartment.

She lived across the waterway from the Plaza and her apartment building was at the top of a hill. The streets in her neighborhood hadn't been plowed yet, and the taxi couldn't make it up the hill, so he had to drop us at the corner.

I held her arm in mine as we walked and caught her more than once when she slipped.

"I miss you when you're not around," she said.

I pressed her against a building and kissed her.

Shoveled snow narrowed the path on the sidewalk near her building so that I had to walk behind her. She had her head down and her hands in her coat pockets. Her skirt showed just below the bottom of her coat. I watched her back and then her legs, the dark tights, the black boots wet with snow. Patches of light from the streetlamps marked the way.

A light snow started falling. She looked up. "What a sad snow."

We fucked until neither of us could anymore. We rolled apart and stared at different walls. Piles of clothes rose out of boxes on her bedroom floor. She headed to the kitchen for water.

I went to the bathroom and took a piss at a lean because of my erection. I put toothpaste on my finger and ran it over my teeth. I took a long drink of water from the tap.

The windowpanes in her bathroom wore wreaths of frost. A small clear spot in the middle of each window let the night outside look in. The radiator clicked.

I stood in her bedroom door. She was on her stomach facing me with her eyes closed. She kissed my arm when I wrapped it around her. I kissed each shoulder blade once, then all the way down her back. I wanted to hear her smile.

"I thought about leaving while you were in the bathroom," she said, laughing.

"I wouldn't have taken much," I said, resting on my back.

She propped herself up on an elbow next to me and ran her thumb over my lips. She tapped her thumb against my lips and went, "Hmmm." We smiled together.

I studied the shape of her face, the blue eyes, the soft hue of her skin, and the dirty blond hair. She looked like a daydream. She blushed and turned her face into the pillow.

"You still can't go," she said, her face buried in the pillow. "Even if you look at me like that."

She turned and smiled, then pulled herself into my arms. I could smell our sex on her skin. I sucked a kiss against her neck.

"Why do we always have to destroy each other?" she asked.

I turned my head away and looked toward the glow of a streetlamp in her window. I turned back to her and she covered my eyes with her hand. She kissed me on the lips. She left her hand there.

"What is this for?" I asked about her hand now covering my eyes.

"I think emotions are made with the eyes," she said.

I found her face with my hand and gently put my palm over her eyes. I parted her fingers and opened my eyes to peek. She did the same.

"We should have at least been lovers all these years," I said.

She looked at my face. Her eyes moved back and forth, searching from eye to eye. "We were a wreck together."

"I always liked you," I said.

"You liked the idea of me. You liked that there was someone just as fucked-up as you."

"That's not true," I said.

"Don't be angry." She covered my eyes with her hand again and kissed me. She sighed against my lips.

"What if it was love?" I asked.

"You're not in love with me," she said. "You're just in love with the idea of me."

I rolled away from her but she climbed on top of me. She kissed me and her hair made a tent around our faces.

"Tell me something nice that I told you," she said.

"When?" I asked.

"When we first met?"

"Do you remember what you said to me after we made love in your car that first time?" I asked.

She smiled. "What?"

"You said, *I have butterflies for you.*"

"I didn't say that," she said, laying her face against my chest so that I couldn't see her.

"Don't take it back."

"It's true," she said. "You know it's true." She moaned sweetly in my ear. "It's still true. Tell me something else."

"When we got back here later that night, you asked me to fuck you from behind."

She laughed loudly. "I do like that."

I tried not to remember the other things. I put a hand over my eyes.

A long sigh set her firmly in my arms. "You can't go."

"Is it because you don't like me?" I asked.

"Oh my God," she said, pulling my hand away and looking in my eyes. "Do you not hear my heart for you?"

We gently tumbled through more of the rough pleasure.

"Fuck me from behind," she said.

When we finished and lay side by side, she covered our eyes with her hands. "Tell me that we don't own each other."

I told her.

"What was your favorite part?" she asked.

"About tonight?"

"Yes."

"When you poked me in the eye," I said.

She hid her face against my neck and laughed. "I didn't know where you were going."

"What was yours?"

"Guess," she said, looking at me.

"All of it."

"Yes," she said, turning to peer at the door.

"Mine too," I said.

She got out of bed with her back to me and put on a white robe. "Do you like waffles?"

"No," I said.

"Well I'm having a waffle."

I dressed and then went to the kitchen and watched her as she made the waffles. She ate at the table across from me. She looked up now and then and tried on a smile for me.

"I wish time was the great healer," she said.

"Time is the softest crime," I said.

"Do you ever talk to your father?"

"Every now and then I'll write him a letter. Were you talking to your father at the end?"

"Yes," she said. "He knew he was dying. He told me he was sorry." She cut a piece from her waffle but didn't eat it. She moved it back and forth in a path of syrup then put her fork down. "But I'm afraid he was only sorry that he got caught."

"Will you ever forgive him?" I asked.

"Time," she said. "You?"

"Time."

She picked her plate up and put it on the counter. She hadn't eaten very much. I stepped behind her and hugged her for a long time.

"You should go," she said.

"I can stay for a little longer."

"I have to finish packing," she said. "I'm leaving tomorrow."

I went back to her bedroom and sat on her bed and finished putting on my clothes. I tied my shoes and glanced around. I ran a hand over the blanket on her bed. There was a glass on her night-stand. There was lipstick on it. I touched the imprint of her lips.

She stood by the front door looking down. She put a hand on my chest, then took my hand and placed it on hers.

"I would have run away with you," I said.

"I know," she said.

"What was all this for?"

"I wanted you to know how much I'd miss you," she said.

The light from the hall came in under the door.

"Kiss me once more," she said.

I did.

"What did you change your first name to?" I asked.

She looked at me.

"Give me something to touch," I said.

She pulled my head down toward hers and looked me full in the face as she whispered her new name.

"I always thought we'd end up together," I said. "I thought yours would be the last name I'd ever say."

I stepped into the hall and closed the door gently behind me.

It had grown colder out, and the snow had stopped. I crossed the street and walked to the end of the block. I turned and looked up toward what I knew was her window to see if she would be there, to see if she might wave or touch her lips with a kiss. But there was nothing except the darkness of an already empty apartment.

And it's been a year and a day and I'm waiting for that phone call to tell me to meet her at the airport. It's been a year and day and what will I tell her when I see her again?

I'll tell her we are our fathers' children. I'll tell her it is love, for the hurt is long in leaving.

I'll say here is your last good kiss when she steps into my arms. I'll say here is the last name you'll ever say.

Then we'll heal all our crimes.

YOU SHOULDN'T BE HERE

BY PHILIP STEPHENS

Midtown

Hodge gave up easy to the yellow at 39th and Broadway, rolling his fossil-gray Futura slow enough to the crosswalk that the driver of the Jaguar tailgating him laid on the horn—some sort of -ologist, Hodge postulated, on the quick to an evening round at Saint Luke's. Hodge waved, his attention fixed, though, on the windowpanes of Gomer's Liquors crowded with decrees set in black and purple ink: *Boulevard Pale, Old Granddad Rye, Boodles*. He thumbed sweat from his upper lip and reached for the radio, gripping a gut of wires before he remembered: safety glass from the driver's-side window leached daily from the floorboard, and cassettes lay scattered—Claude Williams, Julia Lee, Bennie Moten. A Stroh's truck idled beside him.

The passenger's-side hinges squawked, and a woman scooted onto the bench seat and slammed the door. His son, Matthew, would have called her jazz, given acetate and vinyl Hodge had spun for the boy.

"Hey, stranger," she said.

Sweat glistened beneath her cropped curls, and her top clung—salt staining fuchsia fabric at her armpits and abundant cleavage. An ammoniac, loamy odor. Skirt of pleather. Elevated cork sandals were laced to her ankles with denim straps, and a dirigible-shaped scar stood out on her shin. She smiled and lifted tortoise-shell frames, black lenses reflecting the ceiling. Her eyes were dilated. A zircon in her left foretooth glistened.

"What?" Hodge said.

"Seen you coming round. More than once, twice. Don't say you didn't."

"You had a silk carnation," Hodge said.

She patted at her ears. "Shit."

Hodge checked the rearview. A champagne-colored Thunderbird inched toward the Stroh's truck, signaling to slip behind the Jag. "Just getting air," he said.

"Don't y'all soak it through your skin?"

"Sorry?"

"Like salamanders? Pale things in caves? Your air. That's what I figure."

The esoteric knowledge stymied him.

"Buy me a drink?" she said. "For all my troubles?"

"I ain't got that kind of money."

"Gentlemen open doors for the ladies," she said. "Your goddamn door's a bitch. Heard of WD-40? Read up Emily Post?" She crossed her legs.

"We ain't happening," Hodge said.

"Now I'm the real deal." She ran a forefinger down her chest, revealing red lace.

"No doubt," Hodge said.

"You remain to be seen."

The doctor granted his horn full voice.

"Pole ain't gonna turn green," she said.

"Miracles happen."

"When?"

Hodge popped the clutch, squealing from Gomer's corner. At the bus stop south of 39th, a legless man on a rolling platform waved with both hands as if to stop a train.

Hodge had lost custody of his son three years ago, his wife arguing in court that he'd become a threat. Hodge drank. Had drunk. The judge nodded at the close of each of Rachel's tearful stories. He sucked at his bicuspid after she related how one Christmas Eve,

Hodge yanked at the coral-fish bathmat when Matthew refused to sit down in the tub. Suction cups pop-popped, the boy flopping to the porcelain, the blow raising an egg on the back of his head. "You don't sit down," Hodge had said, "you fall." The bump was a good thing, he told Rachel; wounds you couldn't see were the ones that got you. She called him something foul. He couldn't remember what.

The judge didn't much care that Rachel had engaged in liaisons with Hodge's friend and friend's wife for more than a year; both of them worked at the advertising agency where Hodge once endured days in an overpriced warren of egos.

His wife, friend, and friend's wife had recorded their proceedings on VHS—bad lighting, adequate sound—including a blurred scene where Rachel had said "yes" one too many times. Hodge had done video work for the agency, though he preferred the vagaries of print—double entendre, metaphoric marsh.

The judge refused to allow the tape as evidence. Now Rachel shared a condo in Topeka with a state representative who maintained a tidy comb-over and elaborately concealed natural-gas holdings he fed to Koch Industries in Wichita, which, in turn, funded his campaigns. They owned a plyboard mansion in Leawood. She belonged to Kansas. Mission Hills had fluoridated her teeth. The head of Kansas City Southern and his wife were her godparents— Episcopalians versed in the Ecclesiasticus, which didn't apply to them; big in the horsey set, they were. Rachel wouldn't let Hodge near Matthew, and Hodge no longer maintained enough savings to hire another lawyer to roll over and play dead. He freelanced and busboyed part-time at Plaza III, where he labored unrecognized by former clients and coworkers amid remains of chops and steaks. Like Reagan with the Russians, Rachel and her cardiologist daddy—205 angioplasty patents to his name—had outspent him.

To Hodge, Matthew had been a blessed error, his arrival sixteen years after his daughter Lilah was born, and two months before she had driven her mother's BMW inside the garage of a

Victorian off Bell Street, shut the door, and let the engine run. Owners of the house discovered her after they'd returned at two a.m. Often Hodge had cruised the city with Lilah: East Bottoms, where air stank of rendered chicken fat; West Bottoms, its faint evidence of long-gone abattoirs; a grandly deteriorated Northeast, where working girls stalked; lumber-lunkhead mansions in Hyde Park—good to know the ground under you. Hodge had read meters for Kansas City Power & Light to get through college. He'd strode questionable neighborhoods: rats in muddy basements where children slept on bare mattresses; a man who conversed with a taxidermied collie; a woman who'd pressed her naked self to the inside of her sliding-glass door as he passed; gunshots. He'd mentioned once to Lilah how he'd like to live in that Bell Street house. From a desk at the third-floor window, he bet, you could stare down Kansas sunsets or study the sparse skyline of Kansas City—decent, quiet, removed.

"Only madmen work with views," Lilah had said.

"Such as?"

"Hitler," she said. "For one."

"You got yourself educated."

"Your money."

"Your po-po covered a bit."

"You've paid," Lilah said. "Balloons in arteries. I mean, doesn't that strike you as funny?"

"The man's yet to amuse me."

"Prolongs the inevitable," she said.

"We tend to prefer that."

"People are all messed up."

"I take them different sometimes."

Lilah shrugged. "Have to."

He still could not parse why she'd opted to drown on fumes, or in the garage of that house. After he'd quit the juice, Hodge contemplated drowning more than he figured healthy. Gulp and gone, he called it. He liked to watch the Missouri River, no more than a wing-diked drainage canal of silted effluent guarded by cotton-woods and roiling by old-brick and glass-faced buildings. A body could be drowned there and buried at once.

Stroh's turned left. The Jaguar whipped around, and Hodge flowed with a crowd of cars down Broadway. Framed in the rearview, the legless man kept waving; Hodge checked long thighs beside him. Rare working girls had tapped his passenger's-side window with coins; none had gotten in his car. Blame economics; George H.W. Bush; one-in-ten-years wars; crack. If times weren't hard, then, as Lilah might have it, they were all messed up.

"Thirsty?"

"Known to be," Hodge said.

"You sweat like a whore in church."

"Your denomination?"

"Shit," she said. "Buggerèd, blessed, or both. That's church, Honeydew." She took from a fringed leather bag a fifth of sloe gin and proffered it.

Hodge refused the syrup, pulled off below the Record Ex-change, and considered going in for a Ray Charles album that he'd visited, so she'd give up, but he lacked green leaf and didn't want to leave her with his ride. Four car lengths back, the T-Bird drifted to a stop, a blocky headlamped sixteen-footer; its curb feelers shimmered; late light obscured the driver.

She tucked away the sloe gin and took from her bag a Mickey's Big Mouth. Green glass sweat in her hand, and when she passed it over, he caught a glimpse of her pager. How many in her line carted cold booze in purses? He twisted off the cap and sniffed, then handed back the bottle.

"I like the smell."

"What else you like?"

He'd white-knuckled his way off juice, loath to admit to the mad-dening tedium of cold turkey. Writhing on the floor of his rental house off Gillham, he swore truths left his mouth but couldn't determine if they'd originated in his head. He clung to the crapper. He sweat, chilled, cramped, twitched, dreamed, told himself this was but a dream, crying out the child's song for comfort. Scissor-tailed birds scratched along the baseboards of his lathe and plaster shithole, their beaks long and glistening. He killed knots in the hardwood floor.

Hodge lay curled on linoleum tiles of the breakfast nook when a cabal of middle-aged men entered: camel-hair coats, stingy-brim fedoras, brown boots, toes rigged with silver blades. "Out to Hey Hay," the darkest man said, "two bits straighten you out." The others chuckled.

"I want a steak," Hodge said to a square of tile. He thought he might throw up.

"White boy down to Milton's get him a steak. Rare cuts just waiting on you."

He attended one meeting but knew too many people, and his bad habits were not their business, so he drove the city—like with Lilah—riding swells of street as if he were a pilot maydayed out at the controls of a plane gone down in gulf waters.

Hodge rarely thought on the events leading him to quit. He took an elbow from Lou or Hugh or Drew, bouncer nonetheless, and fell against the front door of the Grand Emporium. Onstage, a glistening bald man labored over an Asus7, heavy with watery reverb, the tune bearing no relation to any blues Hodge knew. His shoulder blades pained him. The door didn't give until someone employed a fist to Hodge's face, and his carcass dropped into hard currents.

"Who knows what the drowned have to say," Hodge had said sometimes, "but for the washed up?" Lame pun, and puns were for people, Lilah said, who couldn't be bothered to immerse themselves in jokes, let alone conversations. Patrons set upon him, their shoes fitting gaps in his ribs. They lacked the decency to drag him to a back alley. The owner stepped from his club, worrying his fey soul tag with his teeth, and Hodge crabbed to the curb, asked for air, but tasted blood. An orange Fiesta fumed past.

"Excuse me," someone said; the crowd backed off to reveal man and woman—arms linked for an evening promenade. He wore a navy-blue pin-striped suit, a yellow tie loosened from his starched collar. Her sequined skirt flashed like perch at docksides, and her silver shoes matched—Dorothy in Baum's *Oz*. "Look it up," he'd told Lilah, when at age six she'd requested sparkling red pumps for Halloween. "They ain't ruby." The woman seemed distorted by thick glass—long tanning-booth legs, substantial bust, too-tight cotton blouse. Her teeth were large and bluish. Not long ago she'd played Barbie Ferraris on pressure-treated decks in Lenexa, maybe, a quarter mile from cornfields. She crossed the state line monthly from Johnson County to buy cocaine.

"Oh, hey, Hodge," the man said, stepping over him.

Blood clouded Hodge's eye. The woman smiled. "It's me. Remember? Lilah." She was not Lilah; Lilah was long dead. After that he failed to remember.

For two days of a five-day visit to Truman Medical Center, Hodge lay unconscious. If he'd had visitors, they left neither notes nor flowers. On his third morning, a uniformed cop stood at the foot of his bed.

"Dell," Hodge said.

Hodge and Dell had wreaked mild havoc at Southwest High. They'd streaked the Nelson-Atkins one night, their teenage frontal lobes too underdeveloped to comprehend twenty-four-hour surveillance on grounds where billions of dollars of art were stored. Hodge's father picked him up naked at the downtown jail. Dell's father left him for two days; he'd worked CIA in Indochina four years past the Kennedy assassination. Dell heard his father scream some nights from his parents' bedroom. Now he patrolled Central, but lived over the river—Northland. "Know what goes on down there?" he once said. "I wouldn't run my girls through that."

"Same as anywhere," Hodge replied, but he knew. On a Sunday-morning drive he witnessed one man blow another outside UMB bank downtown; the recipient paid with bagged rock—all while Hodge waited on a light.

"Tip of the iceberg," Dell said.

Dell loved a nervous blond wife, Elaine, who rubbed his thick neck and cooked casseroles Campbell's style. His two girls could sing the score of *Oklahoma!*: everything was up-to-date in Kansas City; they'd gone about as far as they could go.

But now, Dell stepped to the bedside, tapping his wedding ring on the rail. "Told me you weren't quite with us yet."

"That's news?"

"Bruised spleen, three cracked ribs, busted molar, severe concussion, internal bleeding. Here's what I like—four fractured bones in your hand. You hit back, Hodge."

"You gone sorting through my bills?"

"Nurses find it queer when cops ask after juiceheads."

"You weren't my savior, were you?"

"Wasn't even on duty. You plan to press charges?"

"At fists and feet?"

"People attached to them. Know what got you here?"

"Bottom-shelf gin."

"Insulted a woman," Dell said.

"Newscaster," Hodge said. "Half Vietnamese. Fox."

"TV station? Or is that a description?"

"Full hour of fire, murder, and mayhem."

"Folks find it compelling," Dell said. Hat in hand, he scratched his hairline, his left arm sunburned. "Ain't my show."

"I called her a newswhore," Hodge said. He stole a breath that pained him. "Said she instilled fear, encouraged white flight, sharpened needling noses for misfortune. She maintained she did her job; I told her she shits in her own sandbox. She threw a Vodka Collins. Look. I was an SOB. I recall my honest moments."

"Lots of folks like her on TV."

"They like her face; it's a nice one."

"And it's on TV. So you gonna press charges?"

"Against my love of liquor? My smart mouth?"

"Hell," Dell said. "Call when you get out. I'll buy if you keep that piehole shut."

The day faded on him, bed backlit with fluorescent light, window illumined with pollen-yellow dark. Dell had left a cutting of lavender from his wife's garden in a styrofoam cup. Hodge reached for it, hand steady—phenobarbital, benzos, Dilaudid. He'd have to ask a nurse once he tracked the call button.

"Ain't you got AC?"

"Old car."

"How old you got to get for no AC?" Somehow, she'd worked her skirt above her underwear, which was plain white cotton. "I do it all now," she said.

"As opposed to when?"

"You're a funny one," she said.

Cars fled past, watery sounds rushing in, nowhere to stand. He'd swum in the Pacific once, sand shifting underfoot, which unsettled him. The rest of the day he made drip castles on the beach with Lilah while Rachel dived at curling waves.

"I said we weren't happening," Hodge said.

The woman slung her arm onto the top of the seat. A car pulled from behind them, but the T-bird remained, headlights shuttered against the coming dark.

"I got a four-year-old," the woman said. "Want to fuck you some of that?"

"What?"

"Charge you more, but that sweet young body? Honest goodness costs."

"Get the fuck out."

"Honeydew, you need you sweet and pure but can't find it. She do you right, now."

"Get. The fuck. Out of my car."

"Jesus ran with our kind." She drew a forefinger down the back of his ear. "Scripture says."

"Goddamnit."

Already she'd slammed the door, though, blending into blue dark. Legs trembling, Hodge got the car into first. The cassettes were gone from the floorboard; no big deal except for the Julia Lee, a bootleg from Milton's Tap Room in 1949. Hodge's old friend who'd transferred the recording off a Tefifon was dead of AIDS; the lover had finagled through the courts his friend's property, then trashed it.

"Jesus wept," Hodge said. The T-bird floated past him, the prostitute on the passenger's side flicking ash from a filtered blunt. Hodge let out the clutch and eased into the lane. He tracked the silhouettes of risen birds on the taillights.

"You did what now?" Dell said.

"Spent the night."

"In your car."

"North side of what's left of Fairyland," Hodge said. "No numbers on the door. Streetlamps're out."

Dell poured milk onto frosted flakes. Gloria and Georgia had come to the table in pajamas, blue eyes shifting over their cereal. "Darkness makes for good business," Dell said.

"I got to get back there."

"For cassettes?" Dell had his spoon halfway to his mouth. "You ain't got to do nothing."

"If there's some girl—" Hodge glanced at Gloria and Georgia. In a cornsilk-green nightgown Elaine leaned on the kitchen counter, coffee pot in hand. "It's got to be stopped."

"Stop what, Daddy?" Georgia said. The elder at age ten, she called police work obscene; Dell agreed.

"More coffee, Hodge?" Elaine said, but she poured before he answered.

"If—" Dell worked his cereal to the side of his mouth. "Then it ain't your business. If they don't, still ain't. Make it yours, you got a death wish."

"I know the neighborhood. I read a route there."

"Meters? Twenty years ago? Sweet-faced college boy? Over a case of Little Kings once, you waxed rhapsodic about some joint that made urinal cakes on the east side. All because you'd never considered some souls actually had to make urinal cakes."

"What's a urinal cake?"

"Gloria," Elaine said.

"Ain't twenty years ago, Hodge," Dell said. "Know why your piece-of-shit car's missing its antennae?"

Elaine set the pot back on the burner. "Dell."

"He drives it every day."

"Little pitchers," Elaine said. "Big ears."

"Worse on TV."

"Drunk broke it, I guess."

"Crackhead," Dell said. "Needs a pipe to smoke what-all. Crack, smack, the next big thing." He wiped his mouth with a paper napkin, picked up his coffee, then set it down. "Fairyland, right? Chain-linked scrub taking over coasters and rip-off amusements? What was it? Fifty cents to get in? Joint nickel-and-dimed you for everything after. Their double drive-in gave it a go, though. Remember? Skin flicks and Disney." Dell snapped his fingers twice. "What was that ad before they went under?"

"*Fairyland is Fun.*"

"I don't care if you spent a night stargazing and tracking fireflies. Some shit'll be watching you."

Elaine cinched her robe.

"There's a line, Hodge. You know that. Troost. Prospect. It's a gray line, but it's a line. They shoot at EMTs even. God knows what'd come of your lily-white self."

Hodge placed his mug on the table. "Somebody's got to do something."

"You ain't somebody."

Elaine snatched up Dell's cup and dropped it in the dishwater.

"What I mean is—ain't nobody the somebody. Look. You can't know that was just some talk. Weird her working so far off the avenue too."

"Girls," Elaine said. "Go play."

"I'm not finished," Georgia said.

"You can't just hear about something like this," Hodge said.

Pushing back from the table, Dell set his cap square on his head. "You hear worse. It just don't sit in your car and make conversation."

Hodge turned the handle of his coffee cup toward him.

Dell kissed his girls, his wife. He bent over Hodge and kissed him on the cheek, then patted his shoulder twice. The girls giggled, and Elaine shushed them. "Friends do me no good," Dell said, "if they ain't still standing."

Hodge made calls: sex crimes unit, social services, departments of blah, blah, and blah; each conversation curled back on him:

"Now how are you related?"

"I'm not. There's maybe a child involved. The woman stole some stuff; that might be proof enough. You understand?"

"And you have the address?"

"Tags, make of car. What I believe is the address. Empty lots all around, no house number. Didn't you get this down?"

"Sir, there's really not much we can do in this situation."

"Situation?"

"I understand that you're frustrated. We just can't do much with this."

"I've been misinformed," Hodge said. "I thought your organization helped people."

"I'm sorry, sir."

"You ain't the only one," Hodge said.

* * *

He'd run the route six times in three years. So dismal a neigh-borhood no full-time reader wanted it: abandoned houses, copper pipe and wire ripped from walls; roaming dogs, swollen trash bags in alleys; blowflies. It took two hours, though—if he ran—for eight hours pay and offered luminous moments: scent of frying bacon; Howard Tate blasting through clapboards; once, hems of lace cur-tains huffed out an open bay window into a tangle of smoke tree and flowerless lilac, and Billie Holiday sang from a record stuck on a scratch: *Willow weep, willow weep, willow weep—for me.*

Then there was the woman who'd stepped onto the porch as Hodge tromped over Virginia creeper running along a limestone retaining wall. "Excuse me," she called. Down the street a mower started, died. One hand tucked behind her, she wore a flimsy white halter, calf-length jeans. Her hair was shellacked and sculpted. "You the gas man?"

"No, ma'am. Kansas City Power & Light."

"You the water man?"

"No, ma'am."

"Oh, you the light man."

"Yeah. I'm the light man."

She turned her bar top–brown back to him. "Can you tie this?" Down the street the mower sputtered, revved. She pinched the drawstrings of her top between her thumb and forefinger. Hodge glanced around for witnesses. Cicadas squawked from a catalpa.

"I guess," he said. He climbed worn stairs, the woman smil-ing down on him. Behind the front screen a daytime game show blathered from a black-and-white. He sensed someone in the dim back room.

She stared at Hodge from over her shoulder. "How old're you?"

Hodge clutched his meter-reading pad between his knees. He wished she'd step clear of the door. "Nineteen." He tied the strings and hot-stepped off the porch.

"You in a hurry, cutie?" she said.

Near the route's close a green frame house stood. Grapevine

tangled over an arbor at the entrance of the walk; honeysuckle wove through a chain-link fence. Meter in a stone basement. An old woman lived there, vestige of a neighborhood as the developer had intended, and she always insisted he stay for ice tea and a ham sandwich of homemade bread and meat cut from the bone. Hodge ate at the kitchen counter while in a quavering voice she spoke of lost days. Her husband had been a cabinetmaker. "Folks here worked. Not like these ones let their houses go to rot. Can't even mow the lawns. Fairyland back when kept those kind out until they threw a fit at the gates. Before you were born probably."

"I was alive," he said. He tolerated her bigoted rants. People rarely said what they thought.

Once, she took his face between her hands. "You're a good boy," she said. "A good boy."

He was not. Three blocks off Metcalf, on the Kansas side, down a sweetgum-lined street of board-and-bat ranch houses with cedar-shake roofs, Hodge had shouldered open a privacy-fence gate to find a woman laid out naked, oiled and shining on a wicker lounge chair. She sat up, arms across her breasts. "Just a minute," she said, and Hodge shut the gate. When she let him in the yard, a peach-colored bath towel was wrapped around her. He apologized. She pointed to the meter above the air-conditioning unit; peppermint had gone to flower below it.

"Hot," she said as he scratched down numbers, then he turned. Shell-colored combs held up her auburn hair, wisps loose on her neck.

"Yes, ma'am."

"Come in for a cold drink," she said. "Please?"

At the kitchen counter she poured lemonade over crushed ice and added a sprig of mint he had to work around as he drank.

"Thirsty?" She poured him another and stood too close. Her towel had slid down some, and when she let it drop and lifted the glass from his hand, he knew he'd chosen this as the hapless way of his first time. He clenched his jaw to keep his teeth from chattering. He visited the house twice more before one dusk he pulled up outside. She sat at the dining room table, a husband in a blue oxford across from her, a boy on either side. He lost her name, her number; she'd written them on a Wrigley's wrapper.

But the Fairyland route had stayed with him. He drove it four times before he parked outside the green frame house; the roof had collapsed. Thistle, poke, and dock had overrun the yard, and in wild violet at the edge of the walk a gray kitten crouched. The arbor was gone. Hodge toed open the gate, and the creature fled. Palming sweat from his neck, he stepped to the porch as a car crept past, bass line rattling the trunk, theremin whining through the beat. He turned the front door knob, and a cat scrambled over the kitchen windowsill and past the corner drainpipe. Hodge slapped his hand to his chest.

After he passed the house where the T-bird had vanished last night into an attached garage, he parked three vacant lots to the north, screwing his rear- and sideview mirrors for a clear view: small split-level board-and-bat painted brick red, ornate cream-colored ironwork over the storm door and windows, fertilized lawn, clipped grass, edged walk. No bushes or flowers, but a residence that avoided complaints and Housing Authority violations. On his passenger's side a slab stairway led to foxtail gone to seed and flowering Queen Anne's lace and a thick white oak that had once shaded a house. Two blocks ahead stood yellow stucco-coated storefronts, three windows nailed over with plyboard, one intact, a corner joint with a hand-lettered sign over the entrance—POPS SUNDRIES. The door was flaking gray paint.

He'd emptied his bank account—$2,100. If a girl was indeed there he intended to hand over the cash and get her to someone who could help. If Mama made trouble, or the pimp, Hodge would talk his way clear. And if he could at least say the girl existed, maybe the authorities would do something. He might get his tapes back too; who'd want them?

He drank ice water from a Coleman jug. He dozed, sweat; he

stuck to the bench seat. Sometimes he patted the bank envelope of cash in his T-shirt pocket. The air-conditioning unit to the red house ran and ran, and he longed for its cold.

All night the shades stayed drawn. He dreamed a hand touched his forehead as if he were fevered. Mosquitoes raised welts. At blue light he startled, and when sun crested behind the oak an old woman appeared in his rearview mirror. Working a garden hoe for a cane, she shuffled in slippers and an orange robe up the middle of the street, sports section folded in her thigh pocket. At Hodge's bumper, she studied his plate, mouthing letters and numbers, then pointed his way with the tool. She shook her head and moved on into the neighborhood's vanishing point.

At dusk on the second night, the T-bird backed from the garage, and Hodge ducked as it passed, waiting to follow until the taillights turned toward Prospect. He lost the boat at Independence Avenue but checked parking lots of hourly rate motels and cruised from Paseo to North Terrace Park. Waiting on a red, Vietnamese boys in a Datsun with a Bondoed tailfin tossed a lit cigarette through his open window, and when Hodge flipped it back, the driver waggled a snub-nosed .38 at him.

At his rental, he showered, shaved, changed. He drank a glass of milk and brushed his teeth. Come first light he parked at the steps of the vacant lot, but held to his steering wheel as if the car might drift from under him. The old thirst had returned: bourbon, rye, chilled can of Black Label even. When cicadas began squawking, he stepped from the car and headed for the storefront.

A bell pinged. Motes drifted in amber light angling through the window, and shadows shifted in the farthest corner. On his right, the counter led to a polyester blanket nailed over an arched doorway, pale-blue fabric stained down the left-hand side; sixty-watt light illumined the frayed edges. Another shadow shifted, shape of salvaged gargoyle, winged and waiting. Metal shelving ran perpendicular to the counter: chips, Valomilk, motor oil, gardening gloves, Sterno, pseudoephedrine. At the end of one row stood a glass-faced fridge of whole milk, Sunny Delight, and thirty-two-ounce bottles of Bud and Schlitz.

An unshaven man with a monk's fringe of gray curls appeared from behind the curtain. His skin matched the varnished counter. "Goddamnit," he said, and snatched a sawed-off broomstick, whacking it at the door jamb. A brown thing flashed across the far endcaps, tailed by a scrape and a bang.

"Cat door," the old man said. "Wife's cat. Now I ain't got no cat and ain't got no wife—God rest her mendacious soul. I nail it, deck screw it, nut and bolt it; that boy kicks it in quiet as Death. Dorito thief. Nacho cheese." He shelved the broomstick under the register.

"A boy fits through a cat door?" Hodge said.

"Cane-thin. Grease-slick. One big cat too. Was." He scratched at the sleeve of his V-neck. "*Crackbaby*, they call him. Like hell. Baby's a baby. Shit's a shit. Mama's moved on to meth."

"He belong to that house down the street?"

"You hunting something?"

"Cold drink."

The old man waved to a Coca-Cola coffin fridge by the door. Vess cans, tallboys, and malt liquors bobbed in ice water. Hodge hefted a Budweiser, its cold weight a comfort. He loosed a breath, then dropped the beer and fished out a cola.

"Fetch me a black cherry, boy."

"Sorry?"

"Black. Cherry."

Hodge set two dripping cans on the counter and tugged a tube of peanuts from a rack.

"Sit there for days on end, and that's all you eat?"

"I ain't hungry."

The old man cracked his Vess. "What is it you are?"

"I ain't wanting trouble."

"Never matters what you want."

Hodge nodded. "I read meters at this store years ago. Vess was a quarter then."

"Freeway gonna be your Memory Lane soon enough. Tear shit down, lay a road. Improves the neighborhood, they say." The man drained his can. He laid his hands flat on the counter, seeming to study the woodgrain, then belched. "You a cop?"

"No."

"Ain't no geeker; ain't no perv." He lifted his gaze. "You some spook. I see through you to the wall. Best float on out, spook."

Hodge took the envelope from his breast pocket; he held out a five.

"Keep that shit," the old man said. He raised a hand as if blessing Hodge, then pinched up the broomstick and swung it like a pendulum. "You shouldn't be here," he said. He pushed back the blanket, sidestepped the cover, and let it drop. Hodge abandoned the five on the counter.

Tossing the tube of peanuts onto the front seat, he leaned against the driver's-side door, arms outstretched on the hot roof, hands around the can from which he sipped. He watched the house. Behind him undergrowth stirred, and at the opposite walk's edge a calico kitten appeared. Hodge tugged his damp T-shirt from his chest, and the animal vanished as if snatched away. Hodge turned back to his Vess. The boy from the store had wandered into the widespread shade of the oak. Thick switch in hand, he stood amid Queen Anne's lace and foxtail, eyeing the ground before him. He whipped three times at something, then glanced at Hodge before resuming his work, weeds around him trembling with each slice of the air.

The front door of the house opened, and the ironwork swung outward. The woman's face appeared, glistening with sweat. She studied the street toward Fairyland, the lot across the way. "God-damn crazy-ass," she yelled. She shook her head at her shoes. "Freak show," she said. "Dead boys. Rollercoasters." Backing the security door wide she waved to Hodge with a thin scabrous arm, then waved him off. A girl stepped to the stoop: lavender shift with a lace collar; not four, six maybe, seven, a head above her mama's waist. She dragged a Big Wheel behind her like a rag doll, and by the time she reached the walk, the woman had let the iron-work slam, and the door bit shut.

The child boarded her ride, pink flip-flops firm on the ped-als. At the scratch of plastic on concrete, the boy looked up, but already the girl was gone as if into the chain-linked forest of Fairy-land itself. In old tales, lost children left a crumbled trail so they might be found. Hodge took a pull of Vess and set the can onto its sweat ring. The boy beat and beat to the rhythm of Hodge's heart.

Finally, the girl skidded around the northwest corner of the block, legs pumping. Headed for the Futura, she came on, jam-ming the brakes, the fat front wheel punching the slab step. She fixed on the boy, who'd moved to the edge of the oak's shade, and dismounted, taking every other step to the border of the vacant lot. Hodge set his hands at the door frame. She turned. Lilac pol-ish had flaked from her nails. Her frizzed hair was parted clean and off-center, bunched to either side of her head with purple bands. "Why're you here?" she said.

Lilah might have known his mind, but words hooked in his throat. He swallowed hard and put his hand to the cash. "Your mama's got something I want back," he said.

The girl shrugged. "Gets what she deserves." She turned, shift swirling around her calves with flamenco condescension, and stooped, snatching up a stripped limb long and thick as a forearm. High-stepping through alien flowers, she closed in on the boy, who stopped labor long enough to nod. At his side she stood, eyeing him, the ground, him again. Hodge had the can of Vess to his lips when she gripped the boy's downswing. With both hands she hefted the clean limb over her head—her turn.

At Pops the shades had been drawn against the southwest light. Hodge tried the driver's-side handle, but the car drifted from him, the street rising in a swell so high he sidestepped in loose gravel and slipped, near to falling, before he regained ground. Hodge was standing. Hodge was standing, still.

PART II

Crazy Little Women

PART II

THE INCIDENT

BY CATHERINE BROWDER

Northeast

T hey told her the bullet had passed through the right side of her body, miraculously missing any major organ or artery. She heard them but couldn't respond. From the foot of the hospital bed a cheery voice emerged from a white lab coat: "The gods smiled on you, girl."

Girl? She was thirty-four. And what did it matter what was "missed" when the damage felt so enormous?

"You're okay, aren't you, baby?" Juanita was leaning in from the left, her face a blur. Everything was a blur, and her eyes felt bruised and swollen. Ladonna recognized Juanita's voice immediately but was too drugged to register any feeling, even fear. It seemed better not to be conscious or to try to figure out *who* or *what* or *where*. The lab coat hovered near Juanita and then withdrew. From time to time she heard muted electronic sounds, some sort of quiet machinery doing its job. She'd felt safe until Nita's solid frame came too close, blurring what little sight she had.

Someone else entered the room and sat on a chair beside the bed.

"I don't think you should be talking to her," the voice said. A man's. "You're still on administrative leave, officer."

Juanita's shape pulled itself to its full height. Ladonna had forgotten what an imposing person Nita was: solid and broad-shouldered. Ladonna thought it was this solidity that had once attracted her, until one thing led to another. *Love*, Nita assured her. She'd never understood that part of it, understanding instead an attraction to Nita's power and the confidence it gave her. The fact that Juanita was a cop seemed a mere sidebar, but perhaps it wasn't. Perhaps it was part of the package. She'd once joked—*I've fallen for a uniform.* She was never sure Nita found it funny. Nita was so quick to take offense, and she'd wondered if all Latinas were so defensive. She would have liked to ask—an honest question—but was afraid of Nita's reaction. Her own mixed-race parents never showed offense, even if they felt it. They were so cool when confronted, so quick and clever. Ladonna had always strived to be like them and was unprepared for Juanita's volatile response to any perceived slight.

"You don't know how it is, Don," Juanita had said more than once. "It's hard enough being a woman on the force. But being a *brown* woman on the force . . ." Juanita would shut her eyes and shake her head, repeating herself until she'd made sure of Ladonna's support. Ladonna always offered her support, all the while thinking Juanita's people had been in this country for generations and were as diluted as she was. So why couldn't she just get over it? Nita had chosen to become a cop. No one *made* her. Did she think it would be a bed of roses? Besides, from what she'd heard, things weren't all that bad in the PD. They were very careful down at headquarters, wary of discrimination suits. Nita probably took more abuse from civilians than her fellow officers.

"Are you listening to me, Don?" Nita's voice always rose when she told the story.

She gave her stock reply: "I know it's hard. But why torture yourself. It's hard for lots of people." *It's hard for* my *people,* she wanted to say but didn't.

"No, it's not hard for everyone," Nita would answer, her voice growing cold. "It's not hard for your standard-issue male cop. It's not hard for your standard-issue white cop. It's not—"

"I absolutely hear you . . . and you're right."

Whenever Nita started in on the it's-so-hard-for-me speech, Ladonna turned away with a shudder. This might even have been the content of their last conversation before the fabric of their lives unraveled. Just before "the incident." Now her head was a muddle and a male voice to her right was asking questions her mouth couldn't shape to answer. She would like to see his face, but couldn't turn her head. She had a feeling he wore a suit and tie—someone from Nita's headquarters. What could she possibly say until she could remember what happened? Nita must still be in the room because the suit said something intended for her.

"It'd be best if you not come here until we can talk to you both. Alone."

"With all due respect, sir," Ladonna heard the anger in Nita's voice, "Miss Price is like family."

"Officer Juarez, I'm asking you politely to stay away. If you don't, we'll post a uniform at the door."

At least her hearing was in no way impaired. There was steel in his voice. Nita didn't reply, and a slight gap of air opened up in the room. Then somewhere beyond her view, Nita cursed softly and a door swung open.

The suit shuffled some papers. A pen clicked open. A hard surface like a clipboard pressed against the side of the bed, touching her arm, which she could not withdraw.

"I need to ask you a few questions."

Funny, how blunt they were. Not even an apology for the circumstances. Not even the tiniest *sorry*.

"If you can say yes or no, that would be great. If not, shake or nod your head."

No niceties. All business. And how could she answer when she wasn't sure herself?

Would she be pressing charges?

She shook her head.

Did Officer Juarez deliberately fire her service pistol?

Another shake.

Was there a struggle?

A nod.

Could she explain?

A shake. Slowly Ladonna opened her swollen mouth and whispered, "Accident."

The man leaned forward, his ear hovering unpleasantly near her mouth. His hair was reddish blond and clipped short, and she thought she saw tufts of hair in his ear. Acid rose to her throat.

"An accident?" he repeated. Ladonna caught a tone of disbelief. Ladonna nodded and repeated faintly, "Yes."

She learned later that Juanita didn't tell her family for three days. How she managed to withhold that information, Ladonna never knew. Maybe because Nita was a cop, the hospital people took her at her word: *I couldn't reach them.* Much later, the enormity of the lie would take her breath away. When her brother Troy arrived at the hospital, the nurses had to send Nita away because of the shouting. Ladonna could sit up but was still too weak to raise her own voice against theirs. She looked at her brother, swollen with anger and fear, as if he were the older and responsible one, and not one year younger. He'd always been protective, even when they were babies. "Little Ladonna and tall Troy," Nana called them, as if their physical stature described their relationship. Troy was six feet like their father, and Ladonna *was* small—five feet two, smaller than their mother. So small that even today people felt entitled to call her *girl*. Before Troy shot up to his full height, he was fending off anyone who bothered her, anyone at all. From the sandbox to the schoolyard, Troy was there. And he had never liked Juanita.

"Hey, sis," he said, and sat down in the chair vacated by Juanita. He reached his long, athletic arms around her and kissed her on the forehead. Tears stood in his eyes. They might have been twins with their identical hazel eyes, the splash of freckles over a small nose, and what their darker Nana called "café au lait skin."

"What did she go and do this time?" he said

Nita had never *gone and done* anything at all before now. Ladonna shook her head, pinched her eyes shut, and spoke carefully. "Accident. Tha's all."

"Accident? A bullet through your side?"

"Troy . . ." she whispered. "Don't."

"The nurse said you were lucky it passed right through. Missed all the important stuff."

She tried to smile. "I'm okay."

"You don't look one little bit okay to me."

The scowl set in—the famous Troy scowl of disapproval. She knew what he wanted for her, and it wasn't Juanita. He couldn't accept she was "like that" and professed she was "going through a phase," thinking she was "bent" when she wasn't. Maybe she'd had a bad experience with a boyfriend? When he first said this, she laughed out loud. He knew everyone she'd ever been with. He'd never *not* been a part of her life, shouldering his way in whether she wanted him there or not. He'd chased away anyone he didn't approve of, until Juanita. Nita stood up to him, and Ladonna wondered if that wasn't one of her attractions. She couldn't spend her life with a little brother smack dab in the middle, playing gate-keeper.

"You here alone, all these days. It makes my blood boil!"

Since when did his blood not boil? Even Troy's wife Jeri held a brief against Nita. Ladonna had asked Jeri once, as nonconfronta-tionally as possible, "Tell me, do you dislike Juanita because she's a cop or because she's a lesbian? I'm a lesbian too, Jeri. And that isn't going to change."

Another time, when she was at Troy's while Nita visited her own family—no one's family seemed happy with them—Jeri had sniffed over the Sunday roast and said, "Well, the department will promote her quick, won't they? She's a female *and* a minority— they'll get two for one." Ladonna shouldn't have been so startled that this had come from Jeri. To look at her, you couldn't be sure Jeri was black. But the most outrageous remark came from her brother.

"Remember when Liberty Memorial was the gay hookup spot?"

She didn't remember, and neither did Troy. It was before their time. He must have read about it somewhere.

"Police had to cruise because the gays were getting jumped and beaten and robbed. Imagine their surprise if they'd found one of their own up there."

"Lesbians don't cruise that way," she'd told him without raising her voice. He couldn't grasp it, or wouldn't. He kept speaking as if she were just a bystander, as if she weren't gay at all. Besides, if he'd been paying attention, he'd know that Liberty Memorial wasn't the "gay hookup" place of choice any longer and hadn't been for some time. Since it had been refurbished and the museum installed, it was a tourist destination, a future national park.

"How do you explain it to the police department?" he'd asked.

"Explain what? This isn't the army, Troy. They don't care. There's no don't-ask-don't-tell. Okay?"

In her depleted condition she couldn't be sure when the unraveling began. Three days before the incident? A week? The first evening Juanita hadn't come home from work on time, Ladonna went to bed, assuming something on patrol had tied her up. It had happened before. Nita would tell her about it in the morning. Instead, she was awakened at two when a light went on in the kitchen, and she'd heard Nita clanging around: a cabinet opened, glasses clinked, the tap ran, the squeaky fridge door opened and closed. Since their bedroom was downstairs, she heard everything. She got up, pulled on a robe, and went down the hall to the kitchen where she found Juanita making a sandwich. Her movements appeared strange. Sluggish. When their eyes met, Nita's were red and bloodshot. Nita turned away from her angrily. Something unpleasant on the job, Ladonna thought.

"Everything okay?" she asked.

"You went to bed."

"Well, yes. Wouldn't you? I assumed you got tied up."

"You didn't wait up."

Ladonna felt her stomach sink and knot, like a fist clenching. "I'm not following you, hon," she said.

Juanita stared at her and then turned her back, stuck a butter knife in a jar, spread mayo over bread, and slapped the sandwich shut.

"What did you expect?" Ladonna said. "You didn't even phone."

"Am I supposed to check in every little hour?"

Ladonna felt her mouth drop open, and she closed it tight. "Excuse me?"

Nita was drunk, she realized with a jolt. She'd never known Nita as a drunk, had only known her sober, for over three years a stalwart twelve-stepper. It would turn out to be her fault, she imagined, and she felt a hole inside fill with bile.

"I'm going back to bed. You eat your sandwich."

She left the room, her legs weak and shaky. Seeing Juanita this way made her pulse race and her breathing turn shallow. She didn't even want to know the details. She lay down in their bed, rolling onto her side, facing the windows, dreading the moment when Nita came in. Hours seemed to pass before the door opened. Still awake, Ladonna kept her eyes closed, forcing herself to breathe slowly. Nita sat on the side of the bed to remove her boots instead of the little rocker where she usually sat. Deliberately, Ladonna thought. If Nita wanted some sort of consolation, she was taking the wrong approach. Ladonna would not respond.

One by one the boots dropped to the floor. Nita groaned as she removed her leather belt, the police accoutrements, handcuffs and keys jangling as if someone were beating a gong. She dropped the heavy belt on the floor beside the boots. When it hit the carpet, Ladonna felt the vibrations through the bed. The Kevlar vest came off next. Nita grunted as she pulled off her work trousers, and a wave of revulsion swept through Ladonna. Were men this gross? One advantage of being the way she was, she thought, was that she didn't have to deal with the unpleasant physicality of men, their gasses and low-pitched groans and too-hard bodies. But here, in her own bedroom, her partner of nineteen months was producing every pathetic sound she associated with menfolk, and for no other reason than to get Ladonna's attention.

The next day, Ladonna was in the kitchen cleaning her lunch dishes when Nita finally made her appearance. It was noon, and it was Saturday. Ladonna did not need to be at work, but when she saw Nita, she suddenly wished she were there.

"Do you go in today?" Ladonna asked.

"You know I do," Nita said with a curt little bite.

Ladonna put down her dishtowel. "Don't take that tone with me. I put up with you last night, Nita. Don't carry it into today."

Juanita gaped at her. How seldom she'd stood up to Nita because there'd been no need. For nineteen months they'd been considerate with each other. Now this.

"There's coffee," she said, and held out a cup.

A cloud had come into the kitchen with Nita and hung there, dank and poisonous, taking up space. Nita glowered at her and got her own mug off the cup tree on the counter and filled it, leaving a trail of coffee drops across the countertop. Instead of sitting, which Ladonna hoped she would do, Nita leaned against the counter, held the cup in two hands, and blew into it. Ladonna wavered, her desire to get a handle on Nita's problem pushed aside by irritation. Slowly, she picked up a sponge and wiped the spilled coffee off the counter. She wanted to avoid a row, wanted Juanita to share what was bothering her, but even that word *share* had a conciliatory quality she did not feel.

Ladonna pulled out a kitchen chair and sat. "Join me."

Nita wouldn't look at her, examining the exterior of her coffee cup. "Nope. Don't think I will." Cup in hand, she left the kitchen and headed down the hall, closing the bathroom door behind her.

Troy was leaning too close. Everyone who visited hung too close, even Nita and the sergeant from the department who'd come to squeeze out any statement he could. A shiver ran down her arms. How often had Nita returned? She seemed always to be in the room, except when Troy was around. Ladonna thought she'd heard the investigator tell Nita to stay away.

"You're coming home with me," Troy said. "Jeri's already made up the back room. The kids can double up."

Why was everyone telling her what to do? It was almost as dismaying as the way they pushed their faces into hers, nose to nose, thinking she wouldn't hear them otherwise. She didn't want to go home with Troy or hear him go off on Juanita. She wanted to be in her own home. She liked her home, the first house she'd bought on her own, a tidy airplane bungalow in Old Northeast, north of St. John, where she'd been told it was safer. The second story, bright with windows, sat neatly above the back half of the house, like an upstairs sunroom, and she kept her houseplants there year round. It was a sturdy little house made of limestone and brick and stucco. "A popular design in the thirties," the agent had said. There was a maple in the parking area, shapely shrubs along the foundation, a lilac and peonies in the fenced backyard. When she had time she'd put in more flowers. She'd had the stucco and wood trim painted the summer before she met Juanita. Once an old Irish-Italian neighborhood, all sorts of people now lived in Northeast, in all the rainbow colors. She'd bought into the neighborhood for that very reason. Wasn't their president half-and-half, like her? She liked to think she and Nita would just blend in.

When they first met, she enjoyed showing Juanita the area, driving past the mansions along Gladstone Boulevard and up to Concourse Park where kids played in the fountain. On Sunday it was full of mostly Latino families, and she'd driven Nita there deliberately. "Looks like a Mexican zócalo," Nita had said with a snort, taking Ladonna by surprise. It was her first glimpse into Nita's dislike of newcomers. *They should do it the way we did.*

Across from the park, the old Colonnade wrapped around the newer Kennedy Memorial, where Parks and Rec planted cannas and coleus each spring. Copper thieves had recently stripped half the tiles off the Colonnade domes. She was in Juanita's Jeep when she first saw the ravaged roofs. "I don't believe it!" she'd exclaimed, asking Nita to pull over. "Is nothing sacred?"

"Hello?" Nita had replied, and gave her a disdainful look. "You're such an innocent, Don. What kind of world do you think you live in?"

She remembered now: the first bad night had come soon after that remark.

When her brain cleared, she'd know whether she still wanted Nita in her house. At the moment her head throbbed and her side ached. Troy was still talking.

". . . You'll need looking after, sis. Let us do that for you . . . For godsakes, that crazy woman shot you in the stomach!"

His voice lifted up, and she turned slightly and gazed at him, then slowly shook her head. "It was an accident, Troy."

It was her first complete sentence, and the knowledge gave her strength. So she was on the mend. If she closed her eyes, maybe he'd leave and she could catch her breath. *My devoted baby brother.*

"Go home," she said without opening her eyes.

He leaned toward her again, forehead wrinkled. "You say something, Don?"

"I'm okay," she whispered, opening her eyes. "Please go home."

"*Go home*, the woman says." He crossed his arms over his chest and sat back in the visitor's seat. Once he left, she planned to ask a nurse to push the chair away from the bed so she wouldn't have to look at worried eyeballs or smell her visitors' hot breath. At least the medical staff treated her better. Troy would stay until he'd harried her into some concession.

"Don't you think you'll need some looking after?"

He stayed for a full hour more, talking intermittently, circling the room, asking a nurse if there was a doctor he could consult with, reminding the woman he was Miss Price's only close relative who was ambulatory—Daddy didn't get about much and Mama was dead. "I'm the brother and I'm shocked that Officer Juarez is even allowed in this room."

The nurse reminded him that it was Officer Juarez who'd raced her to the hospital and waited through surgery and talked with the medical staff. It was Officer Juarez, the nurse said, who brought what Ladonna might need for an extended stay.

"Officer Juarez did not phone her family," Troy said, his voice growing louder. "It is my opinion, as her brother, that a restraining order should be put on that woman so that she does not come here again."

"You'll need to get the patient's permission."

"She can't give it. She's too drugged."

"Then you'll have to wait till she can. Until then, it's a dead issue."

"That's just it!" Troy shouted at her. "If that *accidental* bullet had been one centimeter up or down, this woman would be dead!"

"You need to calm down, sir, or leave."

He was drawing a crowd. An orderly the size of an NFL tackle approached, dwarfing "Tall Troy." Tears stung her eyes. *Get out!* she thought. *Every last one of you!*

The drugs were wearing off, and as they did the event came back piece by piece and more vividly than she expected. She'd hoped it would not come back at all, that some invisible hand would wipe the memory away, like something erased from a chalkboard.

There'd been a pall over her house since the first night Juanita came home drunk, sullen and full of blame. Nothing surfaced and nothing cleared the air. After several days, they resumed speaking to each other but the air was tainted, like the smoky stench that lingers following a house fire. Then it happened again: Nita came home late, clearly inebriated, or stoned, behaving as if something she refused to identify was Ladonna's fault.

The following day, after dinner, Ladonna made her move: she would not tolerate drunken and accusatory behavior, or the black mood that followed. Juanita had changed and not told her anything at all. "Loving people share their woes," Ladonna said. "And you haven't shared a thing. You glower at me, challenging me to guess what your problem is. *Guess!*"

Nita stared at her in silence.

"What I'm asking," Ladonna continued in a calm voice, "is for you to leave. For a while anyway."

"Leave? What do you mean?"

"Take your things and move out."

"It's our house, Don. Where am I supposed to go?"

"First off, it's not *our* house, Nita. It's my house. You've lived here for maybe fifteen months. Second, I'll give you a week to find someplace to go. Okay?"

Nita cursed and threw the glass in her hand against the fridge. It shattered, and the shards rained down over the floor near Ladonna's feet, one small piece flying into her ankle. Juanita was shouting, "Where am I suppose to go?" over and over. Then words of abuse fell across her head and into her ears, words she had never before heard anyone hurl at her—*bitch, whore, nigger.*

"Who is it? Is it a man?" Nita shouted, eyes wild, her mouth a jagged rectangle. She looked completely deranged.

Stunned, Ladonna did not move. Absolutely nothing in their life together had prepared her for this outburst. "I'm leaving the room," she finally said. "When you calm down we can talk."

Juanita crossed the kitchen in two huge strides and grabbed her arm, spinning her around. "You're not leaving this room. And neither am I."

Spittle blew out of Nita's mouth. She was no longer human, and Ladonna could only think, *Mad dog! Rabid dog!* Adrenalin raced to her head, making it feel hot and light, and she pulled her arm away, yelling, "Let go of me!"

But Juanita grabbed her other arm, holding her as you might a small child, pinning its arms to its sides. Then Nita shook her, and Ladonna screamed, "You're crazy!"

She could not reconstruct it all. It had happened too quickly. She felt herself pulling away, peeling one hand loose, slapping out at Nita. Then an elbow came free, which Ladonna thrust upward to Nita's face, catching her on the cheek. Nita grunted and moved back. When she stepped forward, one hand shot toward Ladonna's head, grabbing her hair.

"Let go!" Ladonna screamed. "You're hurting me!"

"You just hurt me."

She pulled at Nita's fingers lodged in her hair, then took a heel and tromped on Nita's foot, but she was in her work boots. Ladonna gasped: Nita was still in uniform. The realization felt like a splash of ice water. When had Nita become this walking land mine, a cop with an explosive temper? She was scared and couldn't abide the insanity.

"Nita, let's stop this now."

"You started it!" She dropped her grip on Ladonna. "You started it, bitch."

How could she say that to her face? And in Ladonna's own home? Ladonna looked her in the face, flabbergasted, uttered, "How dare you," in a low threatening voice, and slapped Juanita hard across the face. For a long second they looked at each other in the full knowledge of the moment's ugliness. And then Nita's hand dropped to her belt and she unsnapped her gun from its holster. Ladonna felt as though she was watching a bad film in slow motion.

"No one slaps me. Not in uniform. Not even you!"

Her own hand dropped to cover Juanita's fumbling with the pistol. Then four hands pulled and pushed, all of it in so few seconds and in such clumsy mayhem that she would never be able to fully visualize the sequence of events. She wasn't sure she was even watching the gun or their hands but thought she'd shut her eyes in horror, her hands swatting Nita's. When she heard the shot, it only registered as incredibly loud, deafening both ears. Then she was lying on the linoleum, on her back, watching the ceiling turn red. Her side felt odd and began to throb, and when she touched the hurt place, her hand came back wet, as though water were leaking out of her like a broken pipe. Nita was standing over her, screaming.

Then she was being wrapped in blankets, picked up and laid across the backseat of Nita's Jeep, her head swimming, the motion of the truck lulling her to sleep. And when she awoke she was in this place, machinery purring nearby, nurses moistening her lips with ice, and Nita smiling pitifully at her and whispering, "You're gonna be okay. I know you are . . . I'm so sorry, baby. It's gonna be back the way it was . . ."

At the end of the week, Juanita's department sent over their investigator once again. She could speak now, if she kept it soft and slow. And when he asked her, once again, what happened, she struggled to remember what Nita had twice whispered in her ear. *Help me out, Don. Just this once! Please . . .*

"It was on the kitchen table . . . the gun. She was about to clean it—"

"Excuse me," he interrupted. "Was Officer Juarez going to clean her pistol in uniform? They said she was in uniform when she brought you in. Do you recall?"

She closed her eyes and swallowed. Nothing was coming back to her. "I don't remember. I can't reconstruct it . . ."

"Just curious," he muttered, looking down at his notes. "No one I know cleans their service pistol in uniform."

He turned to her, waiting, and she looked away.

"It sounds silly," she said finally. "Stupid even. I picked it up . . . I think I'd just made a joke . . . and she grabbed it back. Thought it was loaded. The gun dropped out of our hands. It hit the table— no, the floor—and fired . . . I was in the way."

For a second their eyes met, and then he dropped his gaze to the clipboard. He knew she was lying.

"Miss Price, you have to pull the trigger. No Glock will fire just because you drop it. You can bludgeon it with a hammer, and it still won't fire."

"Well, it fired . . . Freaky thing . . ." She said it softly, as if she hadn't heard his last remark.

He sighed and mumbled under his breath, "That's what they all say."

She wondered if Juanita was still in the house—*my house!* She imagined Nita going through her things, watching the TV, eating, and sleeping in her bed. *My house!* Juanita owed her. Owed her big time. She was certain now; she wanted Nita out.

Exhausted, Ladonna shut her eyes. The officer was talking to her again. "No," she told him, "I won't be pressing charges." There was no reason to. It was a freaky accident and they were probably both at fault. The sergeant clicked his pen shut. He sighed once more and gave her a penetrating look. He didn't believe her and she tried not to care. He couldn't prove anything. No one could. She felt a chill seep in and pushed the button for the nurse. She needed more blankets.

"Thank you and get well," the officer said. "I'll leave my card with the nurse."

The door opened and closed behind him. No one remained in the room. And what if the nurse gave his card to Nita, would she ever see it again? The nursing staff believed Nita, and liked her. It was Troy they didn't like. She couldn't remember the officer's name. She opened her eyes and gazed toward the window. The shade was partly closed, gently diffusing the late-afternoon light. How peaceful it was. If only it would stay this way: no people, no pressure, no secrets.

She didn't remember falling asleep until a sound woke her. The light in the window had faded to a dull silvery gray. The rest of the room had turned into dusk. She shifted slowly, measuring the weight of her head and the stiffness of her neck. A shadow filled the door, and she gasped inaudibly. When the door closed, she went suddenly cold as though caught in a shaft of frigid air. A medicinal scent wafted toward her, and her body tensed. The odor was faint and familiar but not from the hospital, and her stomach pitched in revulsion. Bourbon, wasn't it? The square-ish shadow moved, and she gripped the sides of the bed, struggling to pull herself up. The shape paused, pulling back into the gloom. Ladonna froze, struggling to bring it into view as her eyes adjusted to the dark. Then a woman's voice whispered her name. "Don?" The shape became instantly recognizable, and her heart lurched, as though an invisible bullet had at last found its mark.

THE GOOD NEIGHBOR

BY LINDA RODRIGUEZ

South Troost

J ames had always said that part of the secret of being a good
neighbor was knowing when to keep your mouth shut. And, of
course, being a friendly, welcoming person. He was working in
the garden, as usual, when the Clarks moved into the house next
door. James went right over, like a good neighbor should.

"Welcome to the block, folks. My name is James Marvin."
With a warm smile, he held out his hand to the husband. He had
to look up to meet the man's eyes, and James was not a short man.
The guy was probably six-five. White with reddish hair. Built like
an athlete.

"We're the Clarks," his wife said, holding out her hand so
James had to shake with her instead. She was tall too, probably an
inch or two over six feet, with skin as medium brown as James's.

He waited for first names, but the two of them turned back to
what they were doing as if he'd already left. So they became just
Mr. and Mrs. Clark.

The house they bought had belonged to the Martinsons, who,
like so many in the neighborhood, had lost it in foreclosure. The
bank owned it for more than a year.

Working outside in his garden, James was glad to see someone
living there again. At first.

The garden was his wife's before she died. Celeste had roses,
peonies, iris, lilies, the classic perennials. She wanted an English
cottage garden. When her cancer got bad, James took over.

In the process, they lost a couple of rosebushes, so he replaced
them with tall purple coneflowers and black-eyed susans. Native

plants that were drought- and neglect-hardy. Summers in Kansas City had always been hot and dry, but they'd been growing hotter and drier, even if idiots wanted to dismiss the idea of global warming. James had been a high school biology teacher before he retired, and native plants had long been his passion.

As he lost Celeste, he lost more of her perennials, as well. When he started trying to rebuild his life without her, he planted butterfly weed, beebalm, and gayfeather. The garden got him through the grieving process. He added more and more native plants and tall prairie grasses and enlarged the garden until it took over half the front yard and most of the back. James saw it as his memorial to Celeste. He felt closest to her when kneeling in the dirt, wrestling with weeds or dividing and transplanting.

His son Scotty lived in Germany, working for the Department of Defense, so he didn't visit often. But Scotty called every weekend. Again and again, he tried to persuade James to sell the house and move somewhere safer.

"That neighborhood has really gone downhill, Dad." Scotty's voice always reminded James of his own father's. It was strange how those things skipped generations.

"It's what it always was, Scotty, a working-class neighborhood. Just the way it was when you were growing up."

"When I was growing up, that head shop and porno place where all the crooks and hookers hang out was a pet store, and the Epicurean Lounge with its armed guards at the door was Eddy's Loaf 'n Stein. The liquor store on that corner was a pizza restaurant. The tattoo parlor was an expensive beauty shop. Mr. Emory's, wasn't it?" Scotty's voice had an edge of sarcasm to it.

"So, businesses have changed along Troost. That's not really the neighborhood." Scotty always tried to make things sound worse than they were.

"Dad, you're one block from Troost. That is your neighborhood."

Sell and move somewhere safer, Scotty repeated. It was an ongoing argument.

Shortly after the Clarks moved in, workmen began digging up Mrs. Martinson's shrubs and perennials and cutting down all their trees. Chainsaws and other power equipment roared for days. James had to leave his house to escape the noise and the headaches it gave him. At the end of a week, nothing was left outside the Clarks' house but grass.

James was appalled, but kept his mouth shut. The good neighbor.

Not long after, he wakened at 4:45 a.m. to a heavy pounding sound and Tony Boll's drunken shouts to his wife to unlock the door and let him in. Tony lived on the other side of the Clarks. Tony kicked at their door, screaming curses.

Suddenly, Mr. Clark's deep voice joined in. He told Tony to shut up and go away somewhere to sober up. James sighed and stepped to the window. He knew Tony wouldn't take that well. Tony threatened to kick Clark's ass up between his ears. Fists cocked, he charged over to where Mr. Clark stood on his front steps in his robe and slippers. James didn't see clearly what exactly happened, but Tony wound up on the driveway, screaming in pain. Clark went back inside.

James called 911 for Tony, and he soon went off in an ambulance.

When Tony came back, his left arm was in a cast and he sported a black eye and broken nose. James was impressed. Tony was a big barroom brawler, and if he ended up with black eyes, the other guys usually looked half dead. Mr. Clark had looked just the same as always.

After they'd been in the house a month and a half, Mr. Clark just disappeared. There was no sign of him for more than a month, then just as suddenly he was back. This became a pattern—several months at home, then vanished for a month or two.

Mrs. Clark developed her own eccentricities. She stood out in her front yard for hours at a time, talking on her cell phone and pacing. When James worked in his garden, the sound of her shrill voice would follow him all over his yard, invading his quiet time with Celeste's memory. When he went inside, he could still hear Mrs. Clark holding forth tirelessly. He admired the long life of her phone's battery.

One day Mrs. Clark's obsessive outdoor phone calls took a new turn. She paced in a long bathrobe, which was tied so loosely at the waist that she exposed her long bare legs clear to the crotch of her red panties. It embarrassed and irritated James. Not satisfied with plaguing his peaceful garden time, she had to invade his privacy as well. She spent hours marching back and forth in that robe several days a week. James just tried to ignore her.

When he told Scotty about it, Scotty decided she was mentally ill. "You need to get out of there, Dad. You have no idea what she might do."

"No, but it's interesting to wonder about." James said that just to work up his son.

"Maybe her husband leaves when she's dangerous, you know. He may know something you don't, Dad."

"I think I'm more worried about Mr. Clark," James joked. "For all I know, he might be a hit man off on assignment. He sure did major damage to Tony Boll."

"Good for him! That damned Tony's needed someone to hand him his ears for years, Dad. You know that."

And so it went. His son and he agreed on very little.

Eventually, Mrs. Clark designated herself as block captain. The block had never had one. Still, she began talking to the city on everyone else's behalf. James just sighed at the arrogance.

One day James received a letter from the city, a warning that cited "*tall, noxious weeds.*" His beautiful purple coneflowers? His prairie grasses?

He called the number on the notice and tried to explain about his native plants. The city guy said a neighbor had complained, and the plants would have to be cut down. City ordinance. Any plant over twelve inches tall, other than trees, could be cited as too tall and noxious. James's neighbors had the right to expect a well-maintained lawn to keep housing values high, he said. And if James didn't cut down the "weeds" and put in grass, another neighbor complaint would lead to a court summons or arrest.

James found this unbelievable. As if his neighborhood ever had high house values! He went to the library and confirmed the bad news. Same thing was happening all over the country. Cities were throwing law-abiding citizens in jail and bulldozing their yards. He hadn't known he was part of the "native plant movement," but he determined that wouldn't do him much good.

When he approached Mrs. Clark, she was strutting up and down her front yard in robe and purple panties, yakking on her phone. James waited until she hung up.

"Did you call the city to complain about my garden?"

She looked down at him with disdain. "That isn't a garden. It's a bunch of weeds."

"Mrs. Clark, this is a carefully tended garden of native plants. It's much more environmentally sound than your monoculture lawn of bluegrass. I would be happy to educate you about the various plants in my garden. They are not weeds."

"They look like weeds, so they are. Appearance is what counts. Property values drop unless all the houses in a neighborhood have neat, well-maintained lawns." She sounded as if she were quoting from a book. She turned her back and started talking on the phone again. She must have been dialing while they spoke.

James sat in the garden, trying to find communion with Celeste's spirit, but he was too upset, and it eluded him. He wiped sweat from his eyes and went inside to drink some iced tea and calm down. Maybe a little whiskey in the tea, even though he never drank before sundown.

James wasn't the only neighbor Mrs. Clark complained about. A man at the end of the block gave loud drunken parties. They often bothered James, but he tried to tolerate them since they only happened about once a month. Good neighbors know when to clam up. One night, the man had a party going, and a police car pulled up. The cops hammered on the door. The party host stepped out and argued with the cops. Over their shoulders he saw Mrs. Clark, who was now standing in the street, watching and talking on her phone. He flipped her the bird. People started leaving the party, and the man at the end of the block stood out on his lawn seeing them off.

He yelled to Mrs. Clark, "Eat my dick, bitch!" and made thrusting motions with his pelvis. She shook her fist at him before turning and hurrying into her house.

James felt a sense of satisfaction at seeing Mrs. Clark insulted. He would never do that, and he was ashamed of the feeling—for about a minute.

That weekend, Scotty called, more agitated than usual. "Listen, Dad, you have to get out of there. Put the old house up for sale. I checked out that Clark guy who lives next door."

"Now why'd you do that, Scotty? You can't invade someone's privacy like that." Just because Scotty worked for the government didn't give him extra-legal rights, but he never seemed to understand that.

"Well, I had a bad feeling about him, especially after you said that about him maybe being a hit man."

"Scott, I was joking! He's probably a traveling salesman. You don't even know his first name. You probably looked up the wrong guy."

"I had his address and got his full name from the deed." His voice became more confident and forceful. "We run security checks on people all the time, Dad. And he's not a traveling salesman. He's black ops."

That sounded like something from one of those superhero comic books. "What on earth is black ops?"

Scotty's voice dropped into the condescending tone he always took on when he explained something about his job. "He works for one of the civilian security firms we employ to do dirty work for the military and the CIA. Assassinations, kidnappings, etc. This is a dangerous man, Dad."

"Wouldn't someone like that be living in the DC area?"

"Oh, Dad! We contract with dozens of companies all over this country that hire former military personnel. Usually with special forces training. Ex-military guys live all over the country, and they don't have to move. They deploy from where they already live. They're on contract, so why would they uproot their families? But the ones who fly out to do short assignments and then fly back home, they're usually the real dangerous ones. Removal experts. You know," he lowered his voice. "We need to get you out of there."

James could hear the fear behind the imperative in Scotty's voice.

"You put that house up for sale right away. I can help. We'll get you into a condo out there, or you can come to Germany and live with Marla and me, but you need to get away from those people."

"I don't want a condo, Scotty. All I want is my garden. It's all I have left of your mother. I can't give up our garden. I promised her I'd take care of it."

"Dad, Dad! Mom's been dead for ten years. And she wouldn't want you to stay in a dangerous place out of some misplaced sense of loyalty to her memory."

"I hope I never get to the point where I believe that loyalty to Celeste's memory is misplaced. Maybe you can just forget your mother and all that she gave you, but I never will."

James was ashamed to remember he had been so upset that he hung up on Scotty. His own son.

Two days later, he was out among the ditch lilies and hydrangeas, once again ignoring Mrs. Clark's piercing phone conversation and her state of undress, when Derrick Kappell, whose mother owned the house across the street from the Clarks, marched up to her. Derrick ran with the Bloods. Dressed in red—T-shirt, hat, socks, shoes, and hoodie with sleeves tied around his waist.

James didn't have any problems with Derrick. His mother was

a sweet, long-suffering woman, and Derrick pretty much kept his gang activities away from the neighborhood. Twenty blocks further north, it would have been hell having a gangbanger living on the block. Those streets around there were up for grabs among the gangs, and the violence was constant. The death rate of young African American males living thirty to forty blocks north and east of Troost kept Kansas City among the top murder cities in the country.

Derrick grabbed Mrs. Clark's phone from her hand and tossed it into her backyard.

"What do you think you're doing?" she cried.

"What in the hell are *you* doing? Calling the city on me for that expired license plate! That's going to cost me money. And what harm was it doing to you? What business of yours was it anyway?"

Derrick was nineteen. He was six feet tall, so she actually topped him a little, but he was built like a linebacker, thick everywhere with hard muscle. He got right up in her face, and the skinny Mrs. Clark backed away, looking more than a little frightened.

James was glad to see that. She needed to be frightened of Derrick and what he and his gang might do to her.

"Your car was a nuisance. I'm the block captain. It's my job to get rid of nuisances." Mrs. Clark's voice quavered.

"You're the fucking nuisance, bitch!" Derrick's shout moved her further back into her yard.

James shook his head at the woman's stupidity, bringing the city's attention onto Derrick in his home. He wondered what he'd do if Derrick started to beat her up. He didn't like the woman or her husband, but he decided in all decency he'd have to try to intervene. That would be dangerous before and after. James didn't like thinking about it. So he tried to fortify himself and steady his nerves.

"Look at you, fucking ho. I ought to call the cops on you for flashing your skinny cunt around the way you do. Right across from my mama's house. You advertising? You want me to send some brothers your way? Maybe some high rollers? I bet you give good head with that big mouth."

James had never seen Mrs. Clark speechless, but her mouth—it was big—sagged open before Derrick's verbal attack.

"I ought to kick the living shit out of you, bitch!"

James tensed his muscles, not that an old man like him would be much of a deterrent to a pit bull like Derrick, but he could try to slow him down or at least get to Mrs. Clark's cell phone in the backyard and call 911 for help.

"I'm sorry! I'm sorry!" she cried. "But you know the city's going to come down on you if you don't follow the law, so why don't you just do it?"

"The city ain't going to come down on me unless some big-mouthed bitch calls them. You get one warning, ho! Call the city on me again, and you will bleed! You understand?" Derrick roared on the word *bleed*, and James thought Mrs. Clark's gangly legs might collapse at the sound. She swayed a little but remained standing, and James had to admire her stubborn backbone, if not her lack of sense.

"I understand. But you know the city's going to be watching this area. They may come ticket you, and it won't be because I called."

Derrick's voice grew very low, yet it sounded so harsh that James wanted to close his eyes. "If the city or the cops come around my house again, I will know it was you that turned me in, bitch, and I will come get you. So you'd better pray they never show up. You understand that?"

She nodded dumbly with eyes that had doubled in size. Derrick stomped back across the street, and James felt a little faint with the relief of not having to face the gangbanger's violence after all. Mrs. Clark hurried back into her house and didn't come out again the rest of the day.

Still, James thought, the neighborhood was not so bad. Derrick's mom had moved her family out here to get away from the gang violence. She brought it with her in the form of Derrick, of course, but he went up further north with his crew much of the time. The gang tags at the stone wall by the liquor store on the corner warned casual troublemakers that this block was Bloods territory. Now, that wouldn't help if another gang decided to move south and invade, but it kept the day-to-day criminals and punks that hung around the places Scotty worried about on Troost from coming down the street looking for trouble.

Not that James was going to tell Scotty he was relatively safe because he was under gang protection. He could imagine how Scotty would take that.

Weeks went by quietly. The heat grew worse and worse. Scotty called on weekends, and they danced around each other, unable to get back to their old relationship and unsure what relationship they had now. Another little victory for Mrs. Clark, James supposed. She had returned to her front-yard athletic phone conversations. She was always fully clothed, however, so Derrick had made some kind of impact.

On a heat-danger Friday, James took the mail from the mailman and sat on a weeding bench to look through it. He found a summons to housing court. He could pay a $210 fine, or he could show up in court to try to fight the accusation of a nuisance yard. He could even go to jail.

James sat with the paper in his lap for a long time. He was seventy years old. He could call the TV stations and let the city arrest him on camera. How would that look?

Mrs. Clark's voice snagged his attention. On her damned cell phone. James turned toward the sound and found his fist clenching. He wanted to do just what Derrick Kappell had done. He wanted to march up to her and bellow and make her shake with fear. But how likely was that?

James read through the summons again, including all the fine print. That was where he found out they were going to bring in contractors to mow down his garden and charge him large fees to pay for it. It was like telling him they were going to execute him and bill him in advance for the headsman. Celeste's garden. Clear-cut to the ground. His hands shook, and the paper rattled.

He sat in the sun and heat for hours, full of rage and mourning, until he was light-headed. Until a plan formed in his mind.

He took his car from the garage. Scotty wanted James to dump the old Taurus but it had everything he needed. He couldn't turn to Scotty. No, James had to follow his own plan.

He drove around trying to find a working pay phone, somewhere beyond the neighborhood. Finally, he spotted a fairly secluded phone over in Kansas, near a white folks' tennis club.

He put in his money and dialed 311, the city call center. Holding his handkerchief over the mouthpiece of the phone and making his voice as high-pitched and feminine as he could, James made an anonymous complaint about Derrick Kappell's unlicensed car and about the unrepaired wooden steps to Derrick's screened porch.

He hung up quickly, feeling sick to his stomach. When he got home, he was so dizzy from the heat that he went inside and slept restlessly until the next morning.

The dangerous heat wave stuck around. James only ventured into the garden in the early morning and late evening. Even Mrs. Clark reserved her outdoor phone promenades for those cooler hours. The weekend came and went.

Late Wednesday afternoon, James heard shouting and arguing coming from Derrick's house. He saw Derrick leave when some of his gang picked him up. James decided to stay inside, but he couldn't help keeping watch at the window.

At about eight o'clock that evening, a strange car with a rumbling muffler and no plates raced down the street. Someone within fired automatic rounds at Mrs. Clark in her front yard. The Clarks' front windows exploded, their door ripped by bullets. And Mrs.

Clark lay bleeding as the car zoomed off. Mrs. Boll ran from her house, screaming at her husband to call an ambulance.

James went to bed, feeling more than a little ill. All he wanted was the blessed blankness of sleep, but he thrashed around, replaying the scene over and over.

The next day, a police detective came to the door. He said he'd heard James was always out in the yard and would have a good description of the car. James told the detective he hadn't gone out because he was sick from the heat. The guy looked at him pityingly and said James didn't have to be afraid, that the police could protect him. James knew the cop was seeing a helpless old African American man frightened to death of his bad neighborhood. James kept repeating that he had been sick and had stayed indoors.

He really was sick. For days, he could hardly get out of bed. On the weekend when Scotty called, James told him he would sell the house since the city was going to destroy the garden anyway. Scotty was happy to hear his decision and told James to go to the doctor.

On Monday, the temperature reached above one hundred again, breaking a ninety-year-old record. James didn't have the strength or heart to go out in the garden, so he sat in the house until the phone rang.

"You were responsible for the death of Jarene Clark," the voice on the phone said.

James could see Clark that first day as he looked up into the man's cold blue eyes and tried to shake his hand.

Jarene? It didn't seem to fit that energetic, irritating woman.

"I didn't have anything to do with her death," James said. "She angered some rough men in the neighborhood. I imagine it was one of them." James was pleased that his voice didn't waver.

"I know who killed her," said Mr. Clark. "He's already been taken care of. But you were responsible. You set it in motion." He paused a second. "Nice plan."

"I really don't know what you're talking about." James heard his own voice flinch, but thought that could be put down to the natural fear of an old man.

"I tracked down that complaint. I've heard the tape. Definitely an older man's voice disguised as a woman's. I found the pay phone and the security camera at the tennis club that covered the parking lot. I had the time and date of the phone call. You were on the tape, making that call."

James closed his eyes. He had forgotten that sometimes there were worse things than the Bloods.

"What do you want, Mr. Clark?"

"I'm coming for you. You won't know when or how. But I'm coming." He hung up.

James set the phone down with trembling fingers. He couldn't very well call the police. He thought about calling Scotty, but to say what? *Goodbye? I'm a guilty man? I've been given the death penalty? It's revenge, but it's also justice?*

He walked outside, ignoring the heat warnings, and started to pull out the chickweed that had invaded his purple coneflowers the way the Clarks had invaded his life. You could try everything to get rid of it, but the only thing that worked permanently was spraying. If you did that, you were guilty of poisoning the earth and contributing to the death of birds and insects. He watched the butterflies and fat bumblebees flitting among the coneflowers and mints.

In September, there were goldfinches. One tiny bright-yellow bird to each coneflower's seed head. Celeste, at the end, had loved to watch them from the dining room window, each making its flower bob back and forth as it pecked for seeds.

There would be no goldfinches for James this year. No September. Heat or no heat, black ops husband or no black ops husband, James would stay right here. In the garden. With Celeste.

THELMA AND LAVERNE

BY JOHN LUTZ

West 8th Street

There was smooth trumpet music wafting from big rectangular speakers hooked up to a CD player. Sounded like Miles Davis.

"This is anybody's idea of odd," said Kansas City homicide detective Rodney Small. Small was six foot five and 250 pounds.

His partner, Eddie Jarvis, was much smaller and had been a middle-weight Golden Gloves boxer. "Killer" Jarvis, though he'd never killed anything larger than a roach. He had cauliflower ears, and a ridge of major scar tissue over his left eye that made him look perpetually doubtful.

"Count me in with the anybodys," he said, gazing down at the dead woman who'd been butchered with a sharp knife that lay nearby. There was a red-stained white handkerchief next to the knife; most likely it had been used to wipe the weapon clean of prints. The victim had obviously been tortured all over her body with the knife before being disemboweled. Some monster's sick idea of fun.

But it wasn't the body on the floor that got to Small and Jarvis; they'd seen plenty of brutalized murder victims in their years as cops. It was the man on the sofa who made them wonder.

Small was looking at something else. "What's that over there?" he asked, pointing. "That a note?"

Earlier, in St. Louis

Esther Clyde saw her child make a gesture precisely like that of her long-dead grandfather, and that creeped her out. Little things like this sometimes tipped the balance.

And just like that, she decided she'd finally had enough.

Her marriage to Seth, who worked for the state of Missouri in some low-paying job she didn't understand, had long since crumbled. They were no longer living together. Hadn't been for six months. Two-year-old Randy could go live with his father, who'd lost a long court fight for custody, claiming Esther wasn't right in the head. (Like *he* was.) Well, Seth could have Randy now. Esther was going to hit the road with her friend Jenine Balk.

Jenine had suggested as much several times. She hated her boss at Hunter's Tales restaurant, where she was a hostess and the walls were festooned with what taxidermists had made of various dead animal parts. There was a rabbit with a tail like a fish, and a squirrel that had wings, to name a couple. Esther didn't blame Jenine for wanting to get out. The damned place was difficult enough to eat in, much less work in.

It was hard to switch jobs in St. Louis, because it was hard to find jobs in the first place. After a brief phone conversation, Esther had easily convinced Jenine it was time for them to leave together for other, possibly greener pastures.

Kansas City beckoned. It was way on the opposite side of the state, if not the world. Esther had been there a few times, walked around Country Club Plaza, visited a few blues joints that weren't just tourist attractions, learned what good barbecue was. *Goin' to Kansas City* . . . That was what Esther called running away.

When Esther phoned across town to her mother and told her what she was about to do, her mother said, "I hope you know what you're about to do, Esther."

"Nobody knows what they're about to do," Esther said. "Not really."

"You said a mouthful there," her mother shot back, and hung up.

Esther drove her old Ford SUV over and dropped off Randy at Seth's place. She took a few minutes to say goodbye to the kid.

Seth said, "I hope you know what you're doing, Esther."

"I know exactly what I'm doing," Esther told him. *Different strokes*, she thought.

When she drove away, she didn't look back. The past was gone, and only the present and future mattered.

That was the plan.

Right off, she traded in the Ford for an older but snazzier red Plymouth Sebring convertible. The guy she gave the Ford to was going to sell it for parts, and for a little extra cash Esther talked him into going ahead and letting the state think the car had been junked out. It had old Alabama plates anyway. Seth would say she didn't legally own the car if she didn't transfer the title, and she'd paid way too much. She didn't care. Let him try to find her through her car. She had her mysterious ways and reasons.

She drove the car to her apartment with the top down even though the sky looked ready to bust open and rain.

It didn't take her long to pack. She jammed her single Samsonite suitcase into the car's trunk, then swung by and picked up Jenine at her place.

Jenine was waiting out front with *her* single large suitcase. Esther was pleased. The two friends had pledged to travel light and were sticking to it.

"Nice wheels," Jenine said. She was a little on the tall side, while Esther was short. Jenine was blond. Esther was a brunette. Though slender, Jenine was shapely. Esther was slim from top to toe. Jenine wore a constant smile and looked pleasantly distracted. Esther seemed always to be concentrating on some elusive mathematical equation. An insensitive person who used the one-through-ten scale for women would put them both down at about seven. Jenine figured they were a collective six. Esther thought closer to nine, if Jenine would drop a few pounds.

Jenine hoisted her suitcase onto the backseat and climbed into the convertible without opening the door. "You notice it's starting to rain?" she said.

JOHN LUTZ // 141

Esther nodded. Said, "Don't the two of us just remind you of that movie, *Thelma and Laverne?*"

"That title don't sound quite right, but yes, we do," Jenine said.

"Okay," Esther responded. "I'm Thelma and you're Laverne. Our new selves."

"Sounds good to me," Jenine—Laverne—said. "Only I ain't sure about the name."

"Get sure."

"Yes, Ma'am!" Laverne grinned and saluted. "Where we goin', Thelma?"

"Kansas City, here we come."

"Amen!" Laverne said, though not with religious conviction.

The rain picked up. Within a few seconds it ran in rivulets down Thelma's forehead from her short, naturally curly hair.

"Gentlewoman, start your engine," Laverne said.

Thelma did, but before driving away she raised the top on the convertible so they didn't look completely crazy.

She drove out to highway 270, then went north and got on I-70 headed west, toward Kansas City. When they took the bridge across the Missouri River, Thelma thought it was like crossing that Rubicon river she'd heard about, where there was no turning back. Not ever.

The two friends would start new lives under their new names in their new city, and they would date men who were more so-phisticated than Seth or the losers Laverne dated. Laverne could get a job being hostess at a higher-class restaurant for much more generous pay. And if she didn't like it there, she would quit. When either of them had had enough and, for whatever reason, wanted to move on to a more golden West, that is what they would do. What they were was completely free, even from each other.

The rain stopped and the sun came out, just for them. Or so it seemed. The Sebring rattled some but ran smoothly over the pavement, reminding Thelma of a magic carpet. Or the magic of movies, and she and Laverne were the stars. They would live in what they'd make a luxury apartment. They would dine out when they felt like it and shop at the Plaza and live like royalty. To the west lay the queendom of happiness.

All part of the plan.

Only a few miles outside Kansas City, they had a head-on collision with a pickup truck.

The two vehicles barely clipped each other, like a high-speed metallic kiss. The Sebring swayed and swerved but stayed on the highway. The pickup truck went bouncing and jouncing off the shoulder and into some high weeds.

"Fool was goin' the wrong way!" Laverne said, as Thelma pulled over and parked. "Musta come down the off-ramp. Did you see him? Did you see that bastard comin' right at us?" She sounded somewhat shaken, but not unduly so.

Thelma ignored her, got out, and walked to the front of the Sebring, which was idling on the highway's slanted shoulder as if the driver had pulled over there to study a map or make a cell phone call. The left front fender was bashed in and there was a long scrape down the car's side. It was still running, though. The engine was ticking over smoothly.

Laverne grinned at her through the windshield and Thelma grinned back.

When Thelma was behind the steering wheel again, she said, "Let's drive back and look in on that fool in the pickup truck."

"Screw him!" Laverne said.

"That's just what I wanna tell him."

They went in reverse back to where the truck sat almost out of sight in the brush. It was black, dented all over, and silent.

Thelma and Laverne walked to where the driver was seated behind the truck's steering wheel.

The driver wasn't a he; it was a hefty woman wearing a red and white do-rag on her head. Some of the red was blood.

"Damn fool didn't have her seat belt buckled," Laverne said. "Look there where her head banged on the windshield."

The truck's windshield was starred as if it had been struck from inside with a hammer. There was blood on the break in the glass.

"Other one was belted in, but he don't look so good either," Thelma said.

They moved around to the passenger side of the truck and both gasped at what they saw. The passenger was a mannequin wearing men's clothing, including blue jeans, a plaid shirt, and a tan slouch hat pulled low over its face.

"Don'cha get it?" Thelma said. "She was traveling with a dummy so people'd think a man was along and wouldn't mess with her."

"And so she could use the car pool lanes," Laverne said.

"That too."

It was true that more and more women were traveling with artificial male passengers. Dummies or mannequins with obviously male clothing. Real enough at a glance. A safety measure in a dangerous world. Not much help in this situation.

"What now?" Laverne asked.

"I want that dummy," Thelma said.

Laverne glanced back into the truck. "What for?"

"I want it. Simple as that."

"It's got blood on it. From the driver's head, I guess."

"Don't care," Thelma said. "You watch an' tell me when there's no cars comin', and I'll get Henry outta there and put him in the Sebring."

"Henry?"

"I always thought if I got mixed up with a man named Henry, it'd bring me luck."

"Henry it is, then." Laverne moved to slightly higher ground where she could watch the highway. "Lotsa bugs around here," she said, slapping at her bare arm.

"Yeah."

"Listen, Esther—"

"Thelma."

"Okay. That lady in the car is surely dead. Ain't this some kinda crime?"

"Stealin' a dummy? I guess so. Just a misdemeanor, I'd imagine."

"I meant leavin' a dead body in a vehicle like we are."

"It was an accident."

"Still an' all, just up and leavin' like we're doin' . . . Ain't that a crime?"

"Don't know an' don't care," Thelma said.

She leaned into the truck and wrestled the mannequin from the passenger seat, careful not to get much blood on her. The driver's eyes were open, as if she was staring at the speedometer.

"Clear," Laverne said.

Kansas City worked out surprisingly well. Laverne right off got a job waiting tables in a jazz club on West 8th Street. It was in a neighborhood that used to be the old Garment District, and where the aroma of coffee from a nearby roasting plant on Broadway hung in the air. Laverne found she liked the pervasive coffee scent, even if it did soon emanate from most of her clothes. They served more liquor than food at the club, and the tips were good.

Thelma, though she was the one without the boobs, found work as a pole dancer in a place called T&A. The pervasive scents there were booze and stale perspiration. Laverne told Thelma she didn't know she could dance. Thelma said that didn't matter because nobody could dance anyway in the stiff leather outfit the management made her wear. Laverne decided not to ask any more questions.

The two of them pooled their money and rented an apartment in a neighborhood where the odds were okay that they wouldn't get raped or robbed. They had to park the Sebring out at the curb, though, and sometimes kids or somebody wrote stuff on the windows with soap. It was no big deal, because it came right off with a razor blade and a damp rag.

So they were happy enough there, Thelma, Laverne, and Henry.

Sometimes Laverne wondered about Thelma and Henry. Laverne didn't treat the mannequin like a real person, but she did buy him a change of clothes. Even a pretty good gray suit—wide in the shoulders so it looked something like a zoot suit—at a Goodwill store. Taught herself to tie a man's tie.

It did give Laverne the green willies when Thelma would talk to Henry like he was real, propped up there in a corner of the sofa, where he usually sat. Laverne even walked in on them once when Thelma was telling Henry a long story about some guy at T&A who'd tried to stuff a five-dollar bill down her leather costume and got his watch band snagged in some chains. When Thelma gave the watch back to the guy he'd kissed it, despite where it had been. Thelma had told the story to Laverne more than once or twice.

Laverne drove Thelma to work one day and went into T&A just to see the place. It was rough and full of rough people. Only a few of the customers were women. Most of the men looked as if they'd just gotten out of prison. They were staring at the busty redhead dancing around a pole like she was a juicy steak they were about to cut into. Laverne wondered how frail little Thelma could stand it there.

Maybe a reasonably stable home life helped. Stable compared to life at T&A, anyway.

The three of them didn't watch much television other than reality shows, but they usually had a radio playing jazz. They'd gotten fond of that kind of music, and Kansas City was one of the birthplaces of jazz. Laverne wondered how that was possible—*one* of the birthplaces. Thelma always got a big laugh out of it when Laverne pondered that question aloud, and would glance at Henry as if he was sitting there laughing along with her, instead of just sitting there being a mannequin. Laverne thought that in truth his expression was always kind of haughty. She suggested one time that Henry was a bit big for his pinstripe britches, and Thelma got so mad she threw an apple at her that almost struck her in the face.

Thelma saw a classified ad in the *Star* and bought some fella's jazz CD collection and player, with big remote speakers. Soon she began leaving music on for Henry to listen to when he was alone.

Things got stranger from there. Laverne would find odd things lying about the apartment, like a black thong that, so far as Laverne knew, Thelma never wore. Least ways, she hadn't seen it in the wash. And when Laverne looked in Thelma's dresser to see if one of her shirts was in there by mistake, she discovered some kind of weird metal clamps poorly hidden under a stack of folded T-shirts. And one day Laverne noticed a used condom on the tile floor near the back of the toilet.

Laverne hoped Thelma wasn't mixed up with one of those sicko types she'd seen at T&A. Those guys could bruise a woman just with their eyes.

Then she chastised herself. Maybe the guys at T&A were simply normal red-blooded American men. What was that saying about books and covers?

Laverne decided to make a joke out of the condom. "Saw somethin' this mornin' that made me wonder," she told Thelma over a breakfast of coffee and cheese pastries at a nearby Starbuck's. "You and Henry gettin' it on?"

Thelma didn't seem surprised by the question. "Not exactly."

"What's that mean?" Laverne had never really examined the mannequin for anatomical accuracy. Just thinking about it made something slither up her spine.

"I think you better drop that question," Thelma said. "About me and Henry." She stood up, holding both cups. "I'll go get us some warm-ups."

When Thelma returned to the table, they talked about how old Johnny Depp was and who was the best celebrity dancer.

* * *

Life fell into a routine that was at least bearable. Laverne got a raise. Thelma seemed happy enough pole dancing. The two women puttered around the apartment when they were home. The CD player was usually on, Miles Davis and his trumpet. Or Thelma filled the silence humming Miles Davis tunes. Henry pretty much just sat there.

Laverne forgot about the black thong and metal clamps and the condom, until happenstance brought them again to the fore of her mind. She came home early from work one day, and as soon as she walked in and shut the door behind her, she heard a strange noise from the bedroom.

Thelma wasn't supposed to be there. She was scheduled to be working at T&A.

Listening to sudden silence, Laverne stood motionless except for her eyes. Her gaze met Henry's, and his return gaze seemed knowing and amused.

"That you, Laverne?" Thelma called from the bedroom. Her voice sounded deeper, huskier than usual.

"Me!" Laverne called. The bedsprings squeaked. It didn't take an idiot to figure out what was going on here. "Should I come back later?"

"Naw," a man's voice said. "No point in that, long as you're here."

He walked out of the bedroom, a large man with lots of dark hair all over his body. Red and blue tattoos covered his whole left side, including his arm. A black beard and mustache concealed most of his face, and lank greasy hair the same color was slicked back and dangled down to his shoulders. He was totally nude except for the condom that covered his huge erection. It was the kind with a reservoir tip.

"You must be Laverne," he said with a wide grin. He was missing a few teeth up top and it made him look kind of devilish.

At first Laverne couldn't take her eyes off his erection. When she did look away from it, she saw the knife in his hand. It was a long switchblade or gravity knife, thin and sharp.

"This is Henry's brother," Thelma said by way of introduction. She was standing in the bedroom doorway, as nude as the man. Laverne noticed a tattoo on Thelma that she hadn't seen before, fancy blue letters spelling out *DEATH VALLEY* low on her stomach, an inch or so above her pubic hair.

"I didn't know Henry had a brother," Laverne said inanely.

"They was never close."

It struck Laverne that Thelma had been working too long at T&A. Which is when she realized she'd seen Henry's brother before, at the bar of T&A, which ran in a curve at the foot of the stage where the dancers performed. He'd been dressed all in black leather like a biker and was half drunk and doing a lot of bragging.

"I know you," she heard herself say. The words had sharp angles and hurt her throat when she talked.

Henry's brother had a crazy look on his face, but it wasn't the craziest look in the room.

"You mean you know my kind," he said. Again the wide, satanic grin. "I bet you think you know all about me. Got me pegged as the worst kinda asshole."

"No, no—"

"Don't apologize. You're right on the money."

He came at her slowly with the knife held low.

"You gonna hurt me?" she asked.

"Only for a while."

Laverne looked to Thelma for help, but her friend was standing with her hands over her eyes, her painted lips forming an ugly, elongated triangle. Henry was no help either. He just sat and stared, looking faintly amused. Above it all, was Henry.

On fear-numbed legs, Laverne backed into a corner.

"You got no reason to hurt me," she said in a pleading voice.

Henry's brother shrugged and said, "Fun."

* * *

"What's that over there?" the big homicide detective named Small asked. "That a note?"

His partner Jarvis went over and used the cap of his ballpoint pen to poke at a folded piece of paper, only enough so that he could peek and read what was written on it. The CD player was still on a Miles Davis piece, soft and smooth. Neither detective would mess with that or the note until the crime scene unit was finished.

Jarvis read the note aloud, raising his voice slightly to be heard clearly above the trumpet: "*Sorry, Laverne. It's all too much, as you well know. Me and Henry's brother are going farther west together. You and Henry can be happy, I know. Or so I tell myself. Loves and kisses, Thelma.*"

Small nodded toward the disemboweled woman on the floor. "That'd be Laverne."

"Most likely," Jarvis said. He made a motion toward the sofa. "And that might be Henry."

"It's possible. But then, he wouldn't have a brother who ran away with Thelma. And do you think that note of Thelma's was written when Laverne was already dead or dying?"

"Maybe Thelma left the apartment first, and didn't know whoever was torturing Laverne was going to take it all the way."

"Thelma the optimist."

"Who the hell *is* Thelma?" Jarvis said. He propped his fists on his hips and glanced around.

"Who's Henry? And who's his brother?" Small asked.

"Something like this," Jarvis said, "there has to be a reason."

"But not one we'd necessarily understand," Small replied. "There doesn't have to be a reasonable explanation for everything. A logical end to every story." He placed his fists on his hips and unconsciously assumed the same puzzled posture as his partner. "What the hell happened here? And why?"

The two detectives looked at each other, then at Laverne and Henry, as if waiting for answers.

Nobody was talking.
Nobody ever would.

LIGHTBULB

BY NANCY PICKARD

The Paseo

I t took Judy Harmon fifty-eight years to wonder about the other children. Maybe it was the deluge outside her apartment that reminded her of the flooding that summer in Kansas City back in the '50s. Maybe it was the lightning flashing over downtown Detroit that jogged her memory. Whatever the cause, the epiphany struck her all of a nasty sudden while she was doing nothing more than watching a crime show on TV and drinking her supper of wine and more wine.

Oh my God, there must have been other children.

Judy sat up so fast that she spilled wine and didn't care: pink blotch on white pants, new stain on her conscience seeping through to soak her in dismay. Only now, fifty-eight years later, did her unconscious pull a light cord to force her to look—*Over here, Judy!*—at the decaying fly in the spidery corner of her psyche's forgotten basement.

How could I have failed to realize it for so long?

It felt like her boss coming in to tell her she was fired, which he had done last week. It felt like not being able to pay her mortgage, which she couldn't next month. It felt like watching her retirement slip away as CEOs bought yachts and stockbrokers sent their kids to private schools. It felt like when she'd realized that she was never getting married, or having children, or doing anything but working all of her life, and it felt like not even being able to do that now. It was a sinking in her stomach, a sick feeling in her heart, a setting of a match to an unburned pile of regret.

I was a child myself! I couldn't have known!

She defended herself to herself and to the other—possibly other, probably other—children who might have been hurt, might have been scarred, by the man.

Outside, rain plunged down her windows in the same waterfall way it had poured that July in Kansas City. That summer, the Missouri River drowned the industrial districts of both Kansas Citys—the Missouri one where she spent her childhood, and the smaller, poorer one in Kansas. She remembered staring at the frightening water from the backseat of her parents' '47 Chevy. The river made a washing sound, like surf where there wasn't supposed to be a beach. Judy remembered a green car, brown water, and a dull bright sky that looked like the dirty chrome on the car's bumpers before her daddy washed them in the parking lot behind their apartment on Paseo. The air that summer smelled wet—not the fresh, clean wet of ordinary summers, but the wet of dirty dishrags, drowned rats, overflowing sewers. She'd been excited to see the flood, wanted to get near enough to watch it rising up the floors of the buildings, and then got scared when her father inched the car close enough to spy the river's currents. They bubbled ugly brown and sudsy white; they surged and swirled in boat-sucking eddies.

"Back up, Daddy! Back up!" she had yelled in panic from the backseat. That had made her father smile, but he slid the gearshift into neutral and didn't tease the Chevy any closer.

"I swear that river could shoot us all the way to St. Louis!" her mother had said.

Now, fifty-eight years later, Judy berated herself: *I should have told them about that man. Why didn't I tell my parents?*

Judy Harmon picked up her cell phone to call her mother.

Judy was eight years old that summer.

While the two Kansas Citys were flooding, she went to Vacation Bible School at a Presbyterian church on Linwood Boulevard near their home. She and her parents lived six blocks south, on the white side of the city's "color line," 27th Street. Blacks who ventured in that direction generally needed the passport of a job.

Theirs was a block of redbrick apartment buildings and old homes converted into rentals. There was a synagogue catercorner from their building. It was safe to play outside or walk home alone from school in her neighborhood even though it wasn't a rich one. The only bad things that had ever happened to her on her own block were getting stung by a wasp and falling off her bike. Once, she'd watched her mother give a hobo a half-empty box of powdered donuts after he knocked on their door and asked for something to eat. When he left, he had confectioners' sugar on his whiskery chin, as if he'd dipped it in a snowdrift, but she didn't have the nerve to tell him.

There were many things she'd never had the nerve to say.

That day, when she walked to the babysitter's by herself from Bible school, Judy carried an umbrella that was too big for her. She had to fight it to keep it up. Judy remembered feeling nervous when she started out—it was five blocks to the sitter's and she'd never walked so far alone. Her father was at work at the factory, her mother had a summer job at Katz Drug Store. Usually Judy went with a little friend; years later she couldn't remember why she walked by herself that day. She remembered hearing thunder rumble, though. Her too-big umbrella was black with a wooden handle, and it didn't keep her dry. The backs of her calves got spotted with raindrops, her dress clung to her legs, her fingers got wet and slipped up and down the handle so she had to carry it in both hands.

"Why didn't you tell us?"

Judy's mother lived in a retirement home in Arkansas. Judy had just told her about that day in the rain.

"I told the babysitter, didn't she tell you and Daddy?"

"She never said a word."

Her mother was angry, as if it had happened only yesterday. Judy remembered her mother as she'd looked in those years—

young, harried, smelling of cherry-scented Jergen's hand lotion and dressed in a cotton shirtwaist, with hose and pointy high heels that caused bunions and bent her big toes sideways.

"Nobody would have believed me, anyway," Judy said.

"I would have! Your dad would have gone over there."

"But then what would have happened? People would have hated us."

Her mother fell silent.

"You know they would have, Mom, for saying bad things about a churchman. Maybe that's why I didn't tell you—because I didn't want to cause you and Daddy any trouble."

Her mother couldn't let it go. "I can't believe she didn't tell me. You were just a child, and she was the grown-up. And I'm your mother. She should have told me."

The man was white, tall, and thin.

In Judy's memory, he wore black trousers, a white dress shirt buttoned to his neck, with a thin black tie, although she might have invented the tie. As she walked home alone from Bible school she passed another church, where she heard someone call out to her.

"Little girl!"

Startled, she paused and looked left. The rain had slowed a bit, so she could see the man from under her umbrella. He stood just inside an open door. He could have been the minister or janitor, he could have been a deacon. She didn't know who he was, but she had a sense of what he was even though she couldn't name it.

She saw a ladder in front of him.

"Little girl, come help me change this lightbulb."

She glanced up and saw a light fixture above the ladder.

She was an obedient child, respectful to grown-ups, but something inside of her didn't like this. Nobody had ever warned her; nobody ever warned any children about anything like this in those days, but still, she knew.

She shook her head and gave him a small, stiff smile.

"Come in here and help me," he called out to her. "Don't you want to come in out of the rain?"

He wasn't attractive. He had dark hair that looked thin and greasy, which was how his voice sounded to her too. She had a crush on the handsome husband of one of her mother's friends, but this man didn't look like that. She wouldn't have wanted to laugh at his jokes, or take any lemonade he handed her.

She shook her head again. "I have to go."

"What? Come closer so I can hear you!"

"No," she whispered, her heart pounding as she started walking away from him. "No thank you."

"But I need help. It will only take a minute. You should help me, little girl. Don't you want to help me?"

He wasn't much of a salesman, she thought years later, or he'd have known never to ask a question that could be answered no.

She walked faster. Why would a grown man need to have a little girl help him put in a lightbulb? She felt shaky and afraid and embarrassed without knowing exactly why. Nobody had told her anything about sex, but she'd seen her parents kiss, she'd been to an Elizabeth Taylor movie, and she blushed when her mother's friend's husband was nice to her. She didn't know anything, and yet she knew. She wanted to run, but she had an instinct like a little animal that knows that if you run you'll look even more like a rabbit. She walked awkwardly, as if she'd forgotten how to move her legs; she walked quickly, longing for the end of the block, longing to turn the corner and get out of his sight, afraid to look back. She kept her face pointed straight ahead, as if nothing was amiss, as if she didn't think he was scary. When she was sure he couldn't see her any longer, she finally did run, releasing the handle of the umbrella when it pulled against her hand, letting it fly off behind her.

"I was so mad at you for losing that umbrella."

"What if he's still out there, Mom?"

"After all these years? Judy, he's dead by now. Or he's as old as I am." She was ninety-three. "He could have Alzheimer's. He could be in prison."

"I think he was about thirty. That would put him near ninety now. He could still be in pretty good shape. Look at you. You're as smart as you ever were, and you'd still be walking a mile a day if your back didn't hurt so much."

"I want him to be dead," her mother said. "Judy, tell me the truth, are you sure he didn't hurt you?"

"He never touched me. Truly, Mom. He never got close."

"You were smart."

"I was lucky."

She didn't tell her mother there was another Judy, an imaginary one who had developed in her mind over the years, a little girl who obeyed him even though she didn't want to, a child who did go up that walk, who entered the dark hallway and started to climb the ladder, a little girl he grabbed when she was halfway up. Judy thought of her as Alternate Reality Judy. Sometimes Alternate Reality Judy made it home and told her parents and they got him arrested and thrown in jail, sometimes she bit him and hurt him, and sometimes nobody ever saw that little Judy again. She'd had nightmares about imaginary Judy. And now she realized there could be real children, other "Judys" out there, and maybe she could have saved them.

"How's your job?" her mother asked.

"Okay," Judy lied, and then quickly got off the phone.

Two more glasses of wine later, she looked at her calendar, and then she looked up airfares to Kansas City.

This is crazy.

But it wasn't only that she hadn't told her parents about a child molester. It was that she had kept silent about a lot of things throughout her life. She didn't say a word when a popular boy in high school mocked an old black man and called him nigger.

Cringing on the inside wasn't courage, and neither was shame. Sympathy, alone, was not integrity. Moving to Detroit where she was in the minority wasn't anything noble, either; she'd been chasing jobs, not racial equality. She hadn't ridden a Freedom Bus or marched in Selma, or even in Kansas City. She hadn't crossed lines, not literal ones like 27th Street, nor metaphorical ones. Once, she'd had a boss who cheated customers, but she'd never reported him. She'd seen car accidents where people could have used a witness, and she'd driven on. She felt as if she'd spent her life with tape over her mouth, one word written on the tape in black and permanent ink—*coward*. It was why she liked mystery novels with strong female detectives; she could feel their courage without having any herself.

"Little girl! Don't you want to help me?"

"I did help you," she murmured as she clicked her payment through for a flight. "I helped you to keep doing it."

In a rental car she picked up at the Kansas City airport, Judy drove into downtown, and then cut east to Paseo where she turned south toward Linwood. What she saw along the way seemed to confirm what she'd heard: the city of her birth was still segregated. She drove past her old address, but the building was gone. The Presbyterian church was still there on Linwood, but it stood empty, truncated, half of it vanished, leaving only bare ground in the place of three stories of brick that she would have sworn could never fall.

And then, there it was—the corner with the church where he had stood in the doorway calling to her. It was an African American Methodist congregation now, she saw from its sign. It looked as deserted as her own old church. She parked anyway, and walked over to the side door. How many times had she sent Alternate Reality Judy up this walk? she wondered. How many other children had crossed that distance?

"That church is closed."

She turned and saw an elderly black woman coming slowly down the sidewalk. Judy walked toward her.

"Hello. I used to live around here," she said, "back in the '50s." She wanted to defend herself: *I was just a child.* "This was a different church then, and I can't remember the name of it. You wouldn't happen to know what it used to be, would you?"

"Well, it wouldn't have been like this one," the woman said. It wouldn't have been African American, she meant. She looked permanently tired; the circles under her eyes were twice as dark as the rest of her face. "It's been a lot of different churches."

"Do you remember any of them?"

She appeared old enough to remember when she herself wouldn't have been allowed to sit in the pews of any church along the boulevard.

"Not from when you would have lived here. Sorry, I can't help you." She started again on her slow perambulation over the buckling cement. But then she turned back: "You might try looking it up on the Internet, honey. That's what I'd do."

"I did look it up, but I couldn't find it."

"This where you went to church when you were young?"

"No. It's where a man tried to molest me."

It felt liberating to say it out loud to a stranger.

"Lot of that going around," the woman said, with a headshake and a look of disapproval. "Good luck to you, although I don't know why you'd want to find that man again."

"I want to stop him."

That felt good to say too.

"A little late, aren't you?"

Judy felt herself flush, the good feeling dissolving into shame.

"If it was that long ago," the woman said with a shrug, "then I expect God's already stopped that man by now."

Judy glanced up the impoverished block and saw no sign of any deity's beneficence to children.

"Do you know where the nearest police station might be?"

"Police? We don't need no police around here," the woman said, in the tone of a wry joke. But then she raised her right arm and pointed. "Go on up west on Linwood, honey."

At the police station, a young black female officer sent Judy back north to the Crimes Against Children Division. The detective who took her to an office there was also Afro American, also a woman. Changes, Judy thought, and was grateful for them. The expression in the cop's brown eyes blended wary attention with a willingness to listen. "I don't know if the archives go back that far," she said, "but I'll check." Her tight-lipped smile reminded Judy of salespeople who didn't have what she wanted but promised to let her know if anything came in, and then she never heard back from them.

"Why now," the cop asked, "after all these years?"

"It finally dawned on me there might be other kids that he did worse things to than what he did to me. He only scared me. I don't think that was his first time. I doubt it was his last time, either. I just thought, maybe I can still do something. Maybe he's a grandfather now, maybe he has grandchildren . . ."

The cop nodded. "If I find out anything, I'll call you."

Judy felt her hope fall.

They traded cards with phone numbers.

Judy got into her rental car, knowing nothing was going to come of this. She had thought she'd feel better for the effort, even if it was too little, too late, but she only felt worse for trying and failing.

Why did I waste all this money I don't even have?

She was sixty-six years old, alone, out of work, at the limit on her credit cards, soon to be out of her house.

Feeling despairing and adrift, she checked her cell phone and saw there'd been a call from her mother.

"Judy, I've remembered the name of that babysitter," her mother said when Judy called. "Or, rather, I didn't remember it, but I've found it."

Judy felt queasy in the hot car. "I didn't know you were looking for it," she responded slowly, and then tried to swallow away the sick feeling in her mouth. She turned on the ignition and the air-conditioning, rolled down all the windows, and waited for a chance to tell her mother goodbye.

"Well, the more I thought about how she didn't tell me, the madder I got. So I looked for my old phone directory, and there it was. I guess personal phone books have gone out of style now that people have those fancy cell phones to keep track of everything, but I've still got mine from every place we ever lived. So, if she's still married to the same man, her name is still Mary Lynn Whelan, and his name was Sidney, and their daughter's name is Sue."

"Wait. What? She had a daughter?" With her free hand, Judy plucked at her lower lip.

"A year younger than you."

"I don't remember."

"I'm not surprised. She didn't have much personality, and what little there was of it wasn't all that great." Her mother laughed a little. "We called her dishwater girl, because she had a kind of bland and dirty look."

"That was mean of us. Mom, I'd better go."

"If you talk to Mary Lynn Whelan," her mother suddenly blurted, "you tell her that she should have told me!"

"I won't be talking to her, Mom."

But after Judy got off the phone, a breeze kicked up. She was still depressed, though her stomach had calmed down. Curiosity got the best of her, and she looked up Sidney Whalen on the Internet on her cell phone—thinking that the old black woman would approve—and shocked herself by finding the listing: *Sidney and Mary Lynn Whalen*. While she stared at it, she got another call, this one from the local area code, 816.

The detective.

"I made a call," she told Judy, "and I've got you some information on a cop who used to cover that beat, back in the day. Do you want it?"

Judy felt her pulse jump with surprise and anxiety.

"Oh. I . . . sure . . . yes. Thank you!"

"I probably should tell you . . ."

When the detective didn't say anything for a moment, Judy said, "What?"

"He's a mean old bastard, and he says there were other children."

He was old, fat, bad-tempered, cancerous, and unreasonable, and he lit into her the moment she entered his room in his nursing home. He was in a wheelchair, and he said, "Come over here where I can see the person who might have saved those children, and didn't. It was you, was it? You knew what he was doing, you could have been a witness. All I needed was a witness, somebody he'd molested or tried to molest, some kid to say what he did and how he did it, and you could have been that girl, but you didn't do it. Why didn't you? Do you know how many children he hurt after you? Before you? Because of you?"

"You can't blame me for what he did—"

"Of course I can, you goddamned little coward."

She recoiled. He was her own conscience reviling her.

"I was eight years old, for heaven's sake."

"Well, you're not now, are you? And you haven't been that young for how long? Fifty years, sixty years? All that time you could have come forward. All that time you could have done some good. Go away. I don't even want to see your goddamned face. Now you come? Now you say there was a bad man in that church? What the hell good did you think this was going to do?"

"Who was he? Is he still—"

"His fucking name is James Marway, and he is a senile old pervert, vegetating away in the Greenly Nursing Home, and they treat him nice and gentle, instead of poking him with hot irons the way they ought to do, and he doesn't even know what he did to those little kids. I kept hearing about it, rumors, and I finally figured out it was him, but nobody would talk, nobody would accuse him, and there wasn't anything I could do to get him. With you, maybe I could have got him. I could have stopped him, or at least got him moved out of my streets. Get out of here! You're too late, you're too damn many years late!"

She fled, and it felt familiar.

"I'm surprised you remember me."

"My mom asked me to say hi."

Judy didn't know why she was sitting in Mary Lynn Whalen's living room. She barely remembered driving there, ringing the door bell, stumbling over "Hello, I'm Judy Harmon, and you used to be my babysitter." *Maybe I want a babysitter right now*, she thought. *Maybe I want somebody to take care of me and sing me a lullaby and tell me I'm not a horrible person.*

"Well, that's so nice of her."

Mary Lynn looked a little confused as she sat at the opposite end of her very nice couch. Sidney must have done all right over the years, Judy thought, thinking of how her own parents had been upwardly mobile too. In her own generation, people were only moving on down.

Mary Lynn said, "How are your folks?"

"Dad died ten years ago. Mom lives in Arkansas, and really likes it. I'm in Detroit. I had a job in accounting with General Motors."

"I can't believe a girl I babysat is old enough to be retired."

Judy didn't correct the impression. She wondered if she looked as wild-eyed, shocked, and besieged as she felt. Probably not, or this woman, this stranger now, wouldn't have let her inside. "What about your family?"

"Oh, Sid and I are okay, I guess. We lost our daughter, I doubt you'd know about that."

"Sue? No, oh, I'm so sorry. When did she die?"

"Oh, not that kind of lost, although honestly sometimes I think it might be better. I mean lost, as in meth addict, all kinds of problems, prostitution, in and out of jail."

"Sue?" This time the single syllable held a new world of shock.

"I know, who'd have suspected she would turn out like this . . ." She trailed off, stared down at the carpet.

"I'm so sorry, Mary Lynn. I had no idea." After a moment, she said, abruptly enough to feel rude, "I want to ask you about one of the times you babysat for me."

"Okay." Mary Lynn looked up, clasping her hands in her lap.

"I came in late one day, from Bible school. It was raining really hard, and I'd lost my umbrella. And I told you that a man had scared me. That I'd run away from him because he tried to get me to go inside his church."

"What?" Her hostess seemed to pull herself together, and then she startled Judy by laughing. "Oh my gosh, I do remember. Didn't I tell you not to worry?"

"I don't remember."

"Well, I should have, because that was just Sue's uncle."

"Sue's uncle?"

"No, wait, I wouldn't have told you that, come to think of it."

"Excuse me. It was some man I'd never seen before."

"No, I suppose you hadn't ever met him, but yes, that was my husband's brother. I'm sorry I couldn't tell you. I should have, so you wouldn't be scared. He was custodian at that church, and we didn't like to tell people that. So silly. We should have been open about it, but we were embarrassed. If we'd only known the humiliating things we'd have to tell people about our own daughter later . . . Sue wasn't supposed to tell anybody about him, either."

"About him?"

"That he was a janitor."

"Are you sure we're talking about the same man? What was his name?"

"Well, it still is his name, though he has forgotten it." She shook her head. "James Marway was, is, his name, because he had a different father than my husband. Sidney's dad died in World War II and his mom got remarried to Jim's dad. I never liked him very well, to tell you the truth. Jim, I mean. There was just something about him, you know? He always loved children, though. So that was a point in his favor. His own kids are incredibly screwed up, though, so it wasn't just us that ruined our kid."

Her eyes had endless regret and bafflement in them. "I think that's why Sue didn't come home with you that day, wasn't that right? I think she stopped off to help her Uncle James with something."

"Changing a lightbulb," Judy said, her mouth dry.

"Was that what it was?" Sue's mother smiled, breaking Judy's heart. "You really do have a good memory, to be able to recall a little thing like that."

Judy told her everything else she remembered of that day.

She had to see him.

"I'm his niece," she told the nurse in his room.

The overhead light was on, making the room unpleasantly bright, but it allowed her to see clearly the old man under the sheets. He wore white pajamas, and the blanket and sheets were tucked up neatly under his armpits, as if the nurse had just performed that service, and then placed his long arms over the top of them. He looked grizzled, with white whiskers and long strands of white hair over his skull. "He needs a shave," the nurse said, sounding apologetic.

"Don't worry," Judy said, thinking of straight blade razors.

The nurse walked out of the room.

Judy went up to the bed and stared down at him. His eyes were closed, and she wanted him to open them, so she said his name several times.

"James. Jim Marway!"

When he didn't respond, she raised her hand and slapped his face so that his eyelids popped open and he looked around, confused.

"That was for your niece," she told him.

He seemed to peer into her face without seeing her.

"Sue," she repeated.

She was shocked at herself, and then momentarily scared that somebody might have seen her slap him. She turned to check if anybody was in the hallway and shielded her eyes from the overhead light. The part of her that was still scared and reticent felt as if it was crawling to the back of her being, and a new, bolder, furious Judy seemed to be taking over.

She let it in, let it flood her with confidence.

"I hate this light," she said, and then walked over and flipped it off, throwing the room into dimness, and closed the door. "Oh look!" she exclaimed in a mocking little-girl voice. "The bulb has gone out! I think this lightbulb needs changing, don't you? Don't you want to help me change this bulb, little boy?"

The old man's eyes cleared for a moment, and he stared at her with panic. She crossed back to his bed and jerked a pillow out from under his head and then put it onto his face and pressed.

"And this is for the other children."

Just northwest of downtown, where the Kaw River flows into the Missouri and they start riding on east together, there is an overlook that wasn't there when Judy was a child. If it had been there in the early '50s, it would have been underwater. She stood with her arms crossed over a railing to watch the rush of muddy water below.

She thought she remembered the river as having been busy with barges and tugs, but there were none that she saw now. It was as treacherous looking as she recalled, however, full of rough current and dangerous eddies. She watched a big log pop up and down, get caught, sucked under, and then turn up again downstream. It made her stomach feel funny, like being on a roller coaster, as if she'd ever been brave enough to actually ride one.

I'm braver than that now, she thought.

She leaned harder against the railing so she could stare deeper down into the river. In the back of her mind she heard her own scared, childish self, yelling, *Back up, Daddy! Back up!*

Judy put her right foot on the lower bar of the railing.

"I swear that river could shoot us all the way to St. Louis!" her mother had exclaimed that day in the Chevy, during the great flood in Kansas City.

Judy climbed to the top rung and brought her legs over until she could sit on the railing. The bar was slick with moisture, and it was easy to lose her grip

PART III

SMOKE & MIRRORS

PART III

YESTERDAYS

BY Andrés Rodríguez
Milton's Tap Room

Like lightning, Milton was gone. He disappeared as Tom was pulling down a fifth of Tanqueray from the glass shelf behind the bar. Tom had grabbed the gin and saw Milton's face in the mirror reflected among the multicolored bottles, a cigar clamped between his teeth. When Tom turned around the owner had vanished. But not into thin air. Milton's Tap Room was fat with the smoke of Kools, Lucky Strikes, Pall Malls, and the ubiquitous Macanudos, all commingled with smells of beer, scotch, gin, and bourbon. Customers didn't breathe so much as absorb the unbroken gray vapors that furred everything like fog in the middle of the night. Tom, the oldest of the bartenders, surveyed the dimly lit space, with its backlit, cutout panels of saxophones and trumpets hung near the walls, its small tables and chairs and low patent-leather black sofas. He noticed the empty stool by the door.

Maybe he's gone to the head or stepped outside, Tom thought. But several drinks and songs later, the stool was still without an occupant. The cool, dark vibe inside Milton's felt different. An argument broke out at a table in the back, and for the first time in twelve years Tom moved from behind the long wooden bar to break it up. Regulars were amazed he had legs instead of wheels—bowed legs like old twigs and just as thin. For the rest of the night he was on edge, spilling drinks each time the door opened and someone strode past the empty stool.

At closing time, Tom and Myra—the sole waitress that night—looked at each other, unsure what to do.

"Did he say anything to you?" Tom asked Myra as he flipped the last chair on end.

"He just told me some joke about the ether bunny when I arrived. Then I got busy with that group what started the bullshit. Man, were they blotto! What about the till?"

"Take it home with you," said Tom, "and bank it in the morning."

Tom and Myra were trusted employees, but tonight Tom felt uneasy about the money. He walked Myra to her car around the corner and then returned to the tap room. Something was tugging at him. He stared at the rows of LPs above the turntable and instinctively reached for Clifford Brown. "Yesterdays." *Da da da dum, da da da dum*, the bass and piano began, followed by strings finer than rain. Then the trumpet entered, dancing among the tables, swaying here and there, rising, falling, moving beyond the smoke-submerged tap room.

Tom looked away from the photo of Milton and Count Basie at the sound of knocking on the heavy front door. Normally he'd never think of opening once the bar was closed, but his mind was running in several directions at once. Wouldn't Milton use his key to get inside his own bar? Wouldn't he use the back door anyway, where all the employees arrived and departed? Did he forget or lose his key? Or had some drunk simply heard the music and decided the bar was still open? He scratched the record lifting the needle from the turntable.

"Yeah, what?" he said, opening the door a crack, but leaving the chain in place.

A small man in shabby clothes stood on the other side. "Um—Milton Morris?"

Tom held his breath, straining in the four a.m. darkness to see the little man's features. "What about him?"

The stranger stepped back and looked up and down Main Street. As the corner traffic lights changed, his profile glowed phosphorescent green. He was about to leave when Tom unchained the door and swung it open. "Come in."

The little man stepped inside the silent tap room.

Tom closed the door and went behind the bar. "Sit down," he said, pointing at a stool directly in front of him. "What's your poison?"

He sat at the end of the bar and looked around the room.

"No, he's not here," Tom said. "I was hoping you'd tell me where he is."

"Took a powder, did he?"

"Can't really say," Tom replied, annoyed by the question.

"This joint hasn't changed a bit . . . still the same dive after forty years. What are you charging for drinks these days, a buck, four bits?"

"What, are you liquor control?"

"If I was, you'd be in big trouble—reopening after hours, offering booze to a city official . . . This ain't the old days, Tom, when your boss was chums with Pendergast. Things are different. Or didn't you notice when you got back from 'Nam?"

"Get your ass out of here!"

Milton Morris never kept a piece in the tap room because he didn't need to. Nobody had ever tried to hold him up precisely because the old-time city boss Tom Pendergast and his people liked him. But that was then. Now Tom wished he had a .38 in his hand, anything, even a shillelagh. Though he didn't dress the part, this guy talked like a hood. He slid off the stool and faced Tom.

"Your boss better show up before too long, coz he's gonna have to talk with us . . . or else, you know how it is, Tom, shit happens."

That, he remembered, was what every GI used to say, whether he bought it in Vietnam or made it home. Tom accepted that life was a bitch. It left you lying in a rotten mess. Shit happened, all right. You couldn't stop it. Yet the little man's threat reminded Tom that the shit bothered him still. He cared about the regulars he joked with every night, and the music of the tap room that blew through his empty soul, and Milton Morris himself, his only friend, a sort of father figure, though *father* was not a word Tom would have ever said. Nor would Milton, who never had a family, ever call him anything but Tom.

"How do you know my name?"

"I know a lot more than that. I know you can't stand this place. I know you'd like to get out. All the way out. If you're smart, you'll bail while you can, Tom, coz shit happens!"

The little man put his hand in his pocket and deftly retrieved a cigarette, which he lit with a Zippo in one crisp motion with his other hand. Then he pushed the door open and left. As he passed the window, he looked like any bum Tom saw in Midtown—anonymous, ragtag, just another city dog padding along the street.

Tom had worked for Milton Morris twelve years. He remembered the first time he entered the tap room on Main Street. It was 1962. He was still in high school, or rather, avoiding high school, when he found himself walking the spine of the city. At 32nd and Main, he paused in front of a window with blood-red Venetian blinds behind a Miller High Life neon sign and listened to a stream of shimmering notes leaking from within. He opened the door, pulling in the pavement dust.

In the pitch black, his eyes were useless. Slowly he made out a burning red tip moving in an arc, and then a shaded lamp glowing dimly in a corner. Starting forward, his hands instinctively tried to grab hold of an invisible guide. The cement floor, with its funk of booze and tobacco, seemed to rise up under his feet. In this darkness then, as if a curtain was pulled back, he suddenly saw a man right in front of him, sitting on a wooden stool, his arm leaning on a narrow shelf attached to a pole, in his hand a glass of Cutty Sark, two rocks. A dark god made him. Or maybe he was the god of this underworld. His round face was pale as a cave-grown flower—but there was shrewdness in the look. He never got up from his stool, only looked at Tom until a mild smile came over his face, and Tom felt worthy to pass and enter this Hades, this haven.

After weeks of coming to listen to Milton's juke box of jazz records, Tom became friends with the man who had run saloons in Kansas City since Prohibition. Milton idolized the old mob days and the wide-open city, Tom learned, and he had no qualms about minors coming to his bar to hang out and drink. "If you're hip enough to dig the music," Milton told him, "you're old enough to start a tab."

Tom paid his twenty-dollar tab the day he was drafted into the army. From boot camp he went straight to Vietnam, where shit happened every day—to everybody. Guys in his outfit disappeared while on patrol: KIA or captured. A fair number deserted, found their way to Scandinavia or settled down with a woman in some remote part of 'Nam. He often wanted to disappear himself, but where was there to go? Either you came home in a body bag or the jungle swallowed you up. But Tom wished he'd had the balls to disappear. He remembered his friend Silky Jones who went to Sweden and wanted Tom to join him there. Instead, Tom returned to Kansas City when he was discharged, and reentered the life he had made in Milton's Tap Room.

Back home, he was wound tight all the time. He needed to calm himself, to get to the real echelon, so he bartended every afternoon and night, listening to Milton's jokes, stories, and reminiscences. People of all sorts walked through the front door: musicians, mayors, professors, hustlers, rich men, secretaries, and lonely souls. They all came to dig the cool sounds. Every year he watched Milton run for governor on the same platform—legalized gambling; and every year he heard Milton's message to countless bad check writers who drank for free in his tap room: "I ain't mad at nobody."

Tom lay awake in his apartment, remembering his and Milton's yesterdays. He didn't want to remember anymore. It wasn't that he wanted to erase his memories. He simply wanted to prevent them from contaminating the present. But the present wasn't all that good. It was filled with some very uncomfortable things: Milton was gone, Tom hadn't lived his life, and he needed to be mad at somebody or something. At five a.m. he was awakened by the phone.

"Yes."

"Where is he?"

"Hello, Cheri."

Milton's wife was twenty years younger than Milton, a Kansas girl with Turner's syndrome. You couldn't miss her in a crowd—if you could spot her in the first place. She was under five feet but looked like Mae West, with an hour-glass figure, platinum-blond hair, and deep blue eyes. Men fell immediately in love with her, including Milton Morris. But Cheri was no kewpie doll; she was loud, whiny, manic-depressive. Tom called her Bubbles, though never to Milton's face.

"Well, where is he? He's not in his office and he didn't come home and he's got no excuse to go carousing!"

That wasn't exactly true. When Milton hired Sana, a tall, athletic waitress from Finland, Tom told him he was going to ask her for a date. "She's all wrong for you, Tom," Milton had said. The next day Tom saw her come out of the boss's office, pinning her hair back up and zipping her skirt. *I'll be goddamned*, he thought. Could Milton's disappearance be about another woman? What was he supposed to tell the man's wife?

"I don't know where he is," Tom said.

"Whadd'ya mean you don't know where he is? Did he vanish into thin air?"

"I mean, one minute he was there and the next he wasn't."

"You mean he took a powder."

"I don't know." Tom's eyes were throbbing from lack of sleep.

"Well, he wasn't lifted up and taken to heaven, was he?"

Tom began to wonder: was Milton hiding from the mob or from his wife? *He'd better talk with us*, the little guy had said. Did the mob want to take over Milton's Tap Room? What would be the point of that? And Bubbles . . . Tom knew that in one of her manic moods she wasn't likely to be doing housework. She had left Milton twice, ran off to California, though he talked her into coming back home both times.

"Look, Cheri, maybe Basie's in town, you know, an unplanned visit, and the two of them are getting together with Claude, Big Joe, or who knows who. He didn't tell me anything."

"I'm worried as hell," she said.

Tom could hear voices in the background. He couldn't tell if they were real or the garbled sounds from a TV or stereo. "Don't worry," he said. His sympathy sounded hollow to himself.

"I don't like being left alone."

"I'm sure there's nothing wrong."

"Who said anything about wrong? I just wanna know where the hell he is, and why the hell he isn't here!"

"Would you like me to look for him?"

"Call me the instant you know anything."

It was nearly Easter. There had been a torrent of rain for two nights, knocking all the blossoms of dogwood and catalpa to the sidewalk in splurges of color that soon turned black and globby. And in the storm sewers, the spring damage and leftover winter leaves lay together seeping like an undrinkable tea.

Tom asked another bartender to cover for him at the tap room and spent two nights driving around town in search of his boss and friend. On the third night the sky was starless and the streetlights shrouded by a dark nimbus as Tom drove in circles. The instant he thought of rain his windshield began to boil with droplets. A sudden roar filled the air. He looked up to see the collision lights of a low-flying plane diving toward the downtown airport. The sound soon faded, but Tom remembered the thunderous explosion of helicopters and supply planes knocked out of the sky. He snapped on the wipers which squeaked like dying birds.

Parking in front of the tap room at five a.m., he began canvasing the neighborhood. A hooker slowly passed him on her habitual toe-walk up and down Main Street. He could tell she did heroin and cocaine by the living skull look. Ten years before, she could have been Miss Teen America.

The Warner Plaza apartments rose behind Milton's Tap

Room—tall, stiff shadows waiting in cold darkness. A light here and there showed the bedroom or bathroom of an insomniac or early riser. A ritual was beginning, Tom thought, or well under way. Someone was staring at himself in a mirror, shaving perhaps, or just staring, gazing, asking, *Who are you? What do you want?*

He walked past the filling station, porno store, and camera shop, heading north on Main. It rained harder now. He crossed 31st Street. A few yards ahead, the door of the Eagle's Nest tavern swung open. Out stepped the little man in shabby clothes. He turned, saw Tom in the predawn light, then began running north. Tom gave chase, as fast as his gimpy knees would let him, pursuing the surprisingly fleet-footed man to the crest of Main, then downhill, the rain folding as it ran over everything.

At 29th Street he turned east, ran a short block before turning again. He led Tom through side streets in Union Hill, all the while glancing back over his shoulder, a smile flickering in his eyes. "Motherfucker!" Tom yelled with no effect, for his lungs were on the verge of collapse and the rain grew louder.

Tom continued the pursuit. He was approaching a battle fury now. Despite the downpour, he could make out a blur disappearing into the wall of rain, even hear the man's splashing feet as he continued running. He ran flat out, following. Where's he leading me? he thought, trying frantically to visualize intersections, dead ends, and alleys. Then he realized he was heading south to East 31st Street, which moved below the thousand-foot TV transmitter tower—a black iron colossus visible for miles in the city. As Tom zigzagged between parked cars, he saw the little man fly across 31st, still looking back at Tom, his arms out, untouchable. He never saw the eastbound car.

It came over the hill faster than it should. The sound of the impact was smothered like a cry by the surf. The car was already blocks away as Tom staggered up to where the little man lay in the street. The rainwater rolled over him with its debris of leaves, twigs, and gutter grit. A vision swam into Tom's mind—that of a soldier lying in a rain-swollen tank track. "Shit happens," he muttered. He looked up at the tower, whose flashing lights signaled threatening weather. Louder now, the rain seemed to be grinding earth and flesh together. Even in 'Nam, he'd never felt so abandoned.

The police questioned Tom for two hours. During that time he told them everything he could remember between the disappearance of Milton Morris three nights ago and the death of the little man just before dawn. And then he offered more. Tom said that the bum had not only made threats at the tap room that night, but also claimed to have killed Milton Morris himself. Tom didn't think that he was in fact dead, but he was going to help his friend by telling everyone that the owner of Milton's Tap Room had been whacked. Tom saw that the cops were skeptical. The dead man was a zero—no prior record, no mug shot, no fingerprints, squat. Yet they were clearly eager to wrap up this case. Their plate was already full: the River Quay bombings of bars and restaurants that refused mob takeover; stiffs turning up in trash cans and parking lots; and a Southside serial rapist whose tally was approaching one hundred. They didn't like the idea of a mob grab in Midtown, and Tom kept repeating that Milton's Tap Room would make a great front. It had been operating in the neighborhood forever, the perfect spot for drops, fencing goods out the back door, or running a loan business. In the end, the cops were grateful that the nameless little man was out of the way. They thanked Tom for his misguided but heroic pursuit of a dangerous individual and sent him home.

Word got around that Milton Morris was dead—murdered by the mob. His wife decided to close the tap room and move to California. The bartenders and regulars were shocked and confused. Losing both Milton and the tap room was a terrible blow. But soon they decided to throw a farewell party.

For Tom, too, it was all wrapped up. If Milton *was* dead, well, what could Tom do about it? But if he was alive, Tom was pretty sure that Milton didn't want anybody looking for him, and didn't need anybody speculating about it. Dead was as good as anything Milton could be at this point. Tom would probably never know who the little guy he had pursued so feverishly really was. Maybe he was mobbed up. Or maybe he was just a grandiose amateur hoping someone would give him a few bucks to shut up and go away. He felt a little sorry for him now that he could look back on it all, but his curiosity was pretty much played out. Something else took its place.

Mobsters would keep killing each other, he thought, so absorbed in their internecine battles. They didn't see they were all out of glory days and were just marking time until their reign ended. On distant shores, other wars, equally futile, would grind to a similar end. And people would go on drinking in one bar or another, regardless of what happened to a tavern owner—or a bartender, for that matter. Oh, Tom would go to the memorial party that the regulars were organizing for Milton, and he'd listen to the stories he'd heard a thousand times, but it all seemed beside the point now.

They met on Easter Sunday because it was everyone's day to escape—from work, family, God, themselves. Tom had seen these people alone or in small groups for twelve years, but it was different to see them all at once. They were good people, for the most part, but he couldn't help wondering where the years had gone. They would recover from the loss of Milton Morris, but would they recover from the loss of Milton's Tap Room? They would find another bar, all right—they could find a bar blindfolded—but the tap room had given them an identity.

Myra approached Tom soon after the party began. "Know what?" she said.

"No, what?"

"A couple of nights ago, some guy swore he saw Milton buying cigars at Crown Liquors on the boulevard. He said he was asking for Havanas in a Spanish accent. Then last night another guy claimed he saw Milton walking a cat on a leash in Swope Park while humming 'Melancholy Baby.' It was a tuxedo cat, he said, fifty pounds if it was an ounce."

Maybe Milton did take a powder, Tom thought. Maybe he had a lot of things to escape from—his wife, his business, a bygone era. Maybe he realized he could start over and become a different person, not that relic which everybody thought they knew, including the mob.

Tom poured drinks and played records and watched everyone having a ball and bawling their heads off over Milton and his tap room. In the middle of the celebration he slipped away. No one saw him leave, and no one remembered him disappearing. He left through the back door and walked down the alley to his car parked around the corner. It was filled with his belongings, which he'd already cleared out of his apartment. He hadn't accumulated much over the years. With a tankful of gas and a glove box of road maps, he left Kansas City—for nowhere in particular.

Driving through the sad streets he'd walked down every day, Tom could easily see the attractions of the past. Memory is a defense mechanism; it's meant to protect you—from both the painful realities of the present and those of the past. Memory is selective. It's also not easy to fact check. But it was more than that. The great virtue of the past was that it was gone and couldn't hurt you anymore. Well, sometimes it could hurt you, Tom thought, reminded of the toll the past had taken on his own life. But that was the thing. Whether it presented itself to you as horrible or glorious, it was over. You had to go on living, and you had to do it now.

Author's note: This story is based on local history; however, it has been fictionalized and all persons appearing in this work are fictitious. Any resemblance to real people, living or dead, is entirely coincidental.

LAST NIGHT AT THE RIALTO

BY MITCH BRIAN

The Celluloid City

Marty had sold the popcorn machine last week on the condition that it would stay in the theater until closing night. Marty was like that. Always making deals with conditions. I'll do this but you have to do that. It probably made him feel powerful. Claire was cleaning the machine a final time, wiping off the stainless steel bottom of the popcorn bin so it shined and reflected the shape of her face like a fun house mirror, when Rance came out of the projection booth and crossed the lobby to the snack bar.

She turned and smiled: "All done."

Rance looked at the machine. She'd done a good job all right. Better than Marty deserved. Tomorrow whoever Marty sold it to would pick it up, or send somebody and that would be that. Rance bet Marty already had the money in his pocket. Marty could feel like he stiffed the guy for a week. Marty was like that. Rance looked back at Claire, taking in her short black hair, wide mouth, and the tiny stud in her left nostril.

She hooked a thumb back at a box beside the soda fountain. "Candy's all in the box. You want me to unhook the fountain?"

"Naw, I'll get it," Rance said. "I'll lock up behind you."

Rance watched her walk back to the cash register, grab her backpack, and sling it over her shoulder. She walked heavy for somebody so light and thin. She'd be elegant someday but she's still a teenager, Rance thought, even if she is twenty-one. He was twice her age and then some. She could be his daughter but he didn't like to think about her that way.

He walked with her to the glass doors as he had done hundreds of time before, crossing the carpet with its swirling red-and-gold patterns and angular masks of comedy and tragedy. He stopped just short of the door and she seemed to follow his lead, not breezing out as she usually did. Rance felt a little shiver, like they were of one mind. She turned to him and he said, "You want anything?"

She met his eyes, uncertain. He couldn't hold her stare for long and as always when this happened, he shifted his gaze to the stud in her nose. It was hard to look at her when she was looking at him. He liked it better when she didn't know he was watching.

"What do you mean?" she asked.

He knew he'd caught her off guard. It was awkward. "A souvenir. Something to remember the place by."

"What, like a light fixture?" She managed a half-laugh, like she was trying to ease the tension.

He didn't mean for this to be tense. Maybe he'd been too abrupt when he stopped at the door like that. "I just thought you might have wanted something."

She looked past him, scanning the lobby. He watched her and wondered if her skin was as soft as he imagined. He saw her blink and could make out every eyelash. If this was a movie it would be a close-up. A luminous, Technicolor, Hollywood close-up as she gazed across the lobby of gold and red.

She looked back at him. And caught him staring. They both knew. She gave that shrug of hers and leaned toward the door.

"I'll remember it fine. See you round, Rance." And she was out the glass doors.

He turned the lock and heard it click. He watched her unlock her bike from the rack under the neon glow of the marquee. He didn't want to watch her ride off into the night. He shifted his weight and was instantly aware of his own reflection staring back at him: short cropped blond hair concealing gray strands, silver frames of his glasses on his pudgy face, faded Hawaiian shirt. He turned his back on her and headed across the lobby to the double doors leading into the auditorium. Just one more thing to do tonight. One last thing before closing forever.

Rance walked down the sloping aisle of the auditorium, headed for the red velvet curtains covering the fifty-foot screen. He'd opened and closed those drapes thousands of times. He once tried to do the math and figure out how many movies he'd projected here over the past twenty-two years. And then there was another ten before that at the old Fine Arts across the state line in Kansas. And the year before that he'd worked a few months at the Brookside Theatre before it closed. A year later, when it was set to be turned into a nightclub, somebody went in during the middle of the night and burned the place down. Rance hated the idea of it burning, but even worse was the thought of disco music rattling those sweet old columns along the walls and the balcony gutted and turned into a lounge with fake leather sofas and shag carpet. Sometimes the mob did right by this town. Torching the Brookside before it could be spoiled was okay by him. And anyway, this place beat the shit out of either of those.

The Rialto had been built in 1949 and wasn't as flashy as the Boller Brothers theaters that dominated the Midwest in the '20s and '30s. It had no balcony, no atmospheric ceiling with fake stars twinkling down, no mock Spanish colonnades. Instead it had clean, modern lines. The walls ascended forty feet and then seemed to ring the auditorium, circling over the top of the screen with a thin line of satin aluminum. Above it, the ceiling curved gently, enhanced by the white plaster, creating the illusion of being open and infinite. It reminded Rance of a planetarium dome before it filled with constellations. The illusion would be perfect except for the water stains that marred the ceiling from a leaky roof. Insurance had fixed the roof, but wouldn't pay to replaster and paint, and Marty refused to go to the hip for it. "People come to look at the screen, not the ceiling," he'd say. But the truth was that he planned to sell the Rialto as soon as he could find a buyer and wasn't about to sink another dime into it.

The Rialto had been dying a slow death for years. The audience for independent movies was shrinking and the big theater chains were booking those few remaining offbeat, specialty, and world-cinema titles that used to be the bread and butter of art houses like the Rialto. These days a single-screen theater, especially one in Midtown, simply couldn't compete. Marty had hoped to find somebody who wanted to take it over, but in the end a real estate developer who liked the location had made a good offer and Marty had found his buyer. Now he was going make a big chunk of change. And it wasn't just the theater he planned to unload.

Rance slowed as he reached the curtain, stepped behind the plush drapes, and stared at the canisters lined up in front of him. These were Marty's prints. Cans of thirty-five-millimeter films collected here in the dusty space behind the screen. There were several crime films, an art house domestic drama, a hospital comedy, a jazz flick, even a sort of western set during the border war. All were in mint condition and all had been shot here in Kansas City. This was Marty's personal memorial to his hometown. If a movie had footage shot anywhere in the five counties that made up the two-state metro area, Marty had to have it. Movies set in Kansas City but shot somewhere else, like that piece of shit Burt Reynolds–Clint Eastwood abortion, didn't make the cut. Marty was adamant about what was and wasn't worthy of his stash.

He came upon the prints in all sorts of ways. He'd used the *Big Reel* newsletter and then the Internet had made it even easier. But mostly Marty knew people. People who worked at film depots, shipping companies, other theater owners, especially back in the day before things got computerized and corporations got involved. Marty knew people who could get him the movies he wanted. And he squirreled away the prints here, behind the screen. Once in a while he'd tell Rance to thread one up (Marty was all thumbs when it came to the projectors), but more often than not, he just liked having them.

"Closing night after the last show, I want you to put all the prints into your truck and bring 'em over to my place," he told Rance. He'd just dropped the bomb on Rance that he was selling the place and he said it almost like an afterthought. He'd given no warning. Hadn't even hinted he was looking for a buyer. After all, Rance was just the projectionist. Marty probably figured he'd find another job easily enough. Or maybe just do something else. Everything was going digital anyway. Projectionists, he'd joked, were a dying breed. It may have been funny to Marty, but not to Rance. It was the truth. Rance was dying. He'd kept that from Marty. Same way Marty'd kept the news of the sale from Rance. It wouldn't do any good to tell Marty, anyway. Marty didn't give a shit. He offered no health insurance to employees and what he paid Rance wasn't enough to afford the premiums. Not that Rance cared about insurance. At least not initially. He'd always been healthy as a horse. He didn't smoke, he ate right, and he walked to work no matter what the weather. He'd thought he was in pretty good shape until he started feeling lousy and finally bit the bullet to get his first physical in fifteen years, so the spot on his lung came as a helluva shock. Even worse was how little could be done. And then the news he was soon to be out of a job—devastating. So now Marty didn't know Rance was sick. Marty didn't know Rance had nothing to lose. Marty didn't know how danger-ous Rance was about to become. These prints were not going to Rance's truck.

He reached down and grabbed the closest print, two steel can-isters containing *Bucktown*, a blaxploitation number starring Fred "The Hammer" Williamson. This was the first print Marty had got hold of. The one that started the collection. Nobody'd figure Marty for this kind of low-rent stuff. You could barely see the Kan-sas City locations in it because it took place mostly at night and was too goddamned dark to see anything besides an occasional street corner. But then Rance heard the story—Marty got a blow-job from a nightclub-scene extra called Roxie—and realized the guy's interest in the print was sentimental. It was his memento of the wild 1970s. Like the face that launched a thousand ships, Roxie's blowjob launched Marty's collection.

Rance knew the collection was under way when Marty proudly told him he'd been given a print of *Kansas City Bomber* the night after he'd salvaged a print of *The Delinquents* from a dumpster behind the old Calvin Film Studio.

Rance remembered seeing *Kansas City Bomber* for a buck and a quarter at the Capri's twilight show. Even though people said Raquel Welch had shot some scenes in Kansas City, Rance sure couldn't spot them. Marty said they must have been cut out and kept the print despite his shot-in-town criteria. It wasn't much of a picture but it did have the MGM lion at the beginning and Rance loved the way it reverberated in the cavernous space of the Rialto. Rance loved the sound of that roar.

The Delinquents, on the other hand, had some nice car cruising scenes, especially in the credits, and you could see what downtown looked like back when the streets were lit up with countless bars and strip clubs.

The Cool and the Crazy had even better location scenes, including a sweet shot of the Indian statue overlooking the city, and Marty had snatched up a print of that not long after getting *The Delinquents*. Too bad he'll never get to see it again, thought Rance as he reached the lobby and turned to the door marked with white-stenciled letters: *Employees Only*. He pushed through the door and went inside.

Rance carried the print into the projection booth. The electrical box was buzzing its constant tone that always grated on Marty but made Rance feel at home. For all intents and purposes, this *was* Rance's home. He'd worked here, ate here, drank, fucked (only once), and occasionally slept here for over two decades. The place was lovingly hung with posters. And there were a few real collector's items—a framed letter from Stanley Kubrick with instructions on the projection of *Barry Lyndon*—that had been passed down to him from Uncle Frank. Beyond the 1980s platter system, the splicing bench sat against the back wall, immaculate and organized for maximum efficiency. There were white editor's gloves but Rance never used them. He liked to feel the edges of the film against his fingertips. He liked holding the film up to the light to see the images. He liked the smell of the stuff. A corny, hand-painted plaque hung over the table saying, *Old Projectionists never die, they just FADE OUT*. It was hard to believe this was his last night in here.

This was where it all happened. Up here in the booth. No projectionist, no movie. He was the last link in the chain from concept to script to production to post. It all climaxed up here with him. You can keep your movie stars. The projectionists were the real heroes of the pictures. The secret heroes who fixed whether a movie lived or died, whether it was hated or loved. He'd heard all the stories. How the guy showing *Bonnie and Clyde* had turned down the volume during the gunshots so it was all nice and even . . . and nearly been fired for it. Or how a civic-minded projectionist working a drive-in show in Kansas had said, "No smut here," and cut out the vile scene in *Midnight Express* when the girl shoved her titties up against the glass. Rance didn't blame him. If he'd directed that movie he'd have skipped all that shit in the middle and got right to the escape and revenge and spent a little more time torturing those fucking Turkish prison guards.

Even better was what had happened when *Prime Cut* premiered over in Lawrence during the heyday of the hippies and student radicals. Marty had a print of *Prime Cut* because a lot of it was shot around the stockyards in the West Bottoms, at the Muehlebach Hotel and along the Missouri River. But the big chase scene was shot outside Lawrence at the Douglas County Fair. When the sequence started up and Lee Marvin was rescuing Sissy Spacek, there was the local sheriff, ol' Rex Johnson himself, up on the screen. The hippies in the audience roared with laughter. They booed and jeered like *he* was the villain, not Gene Hackman. Somebody even threw popcorn. It was a disaster. The hippies had ruined the show. Before the next showing took place, the projectionist snipped the sheriff out of the print and the movie went just fine. He showed those fucking hippies who was running things. He saved the movie. Up in the booth, the projectionist was king. Here at the Rialto, Rance was king. And like a king, the title of projectionist had been passed down to him when he was still a boy.

His Uncle Frank had been a union projectionist since the '50s. Rance was six when Uncle Frank stepped in to help his mom after the old man walked out. Frank was better than a father because he wasn't around all the time, only when you needed him. He let Rance into the booth all the time, but the really big thing happened when he was eight and he went with Frank to the Royal to see a preview screening being projected by Frank's buddy Walt. Rance and Frank slipped into the booth just before the show started and Rance sat on a stool, boosted up by a phone book, and watched the movie through a small glass window.

The movie was *The Wild Bunch*. It was the bloodiest, dirtiest, most beautiful thing he'd ever seen. The theater was packed with people expecting to see a Hollywood western with movie stars like William Holden and Ernest Borgnine. There was a national teacher's convention going on that week and dozens of ladies, in town for the weekend, had been given complimentary tickets. There were hippies too. Uncle Frank had pointed them out to Rance as they moved through the crowded lobby. Hippies taking a break from smoking dope or burning American flags. Hippies hoping to get out of the heat, putting their grimy feet up on the seats in front of them and making fun of a cowboy movie.

Boy, did they get a surprise. Once the bunch started shooting the shit out of the town of Starbuck, people started leaving the theater. With every gunshot, every glorious eruption of crimson, every slow-motion tumble, another one would leave. One of the teachers let out a scream when a woman was shot in the back. Another tripped and fell in the aisle, trying to get out before Crazy Lee's tongue went all the way inside that old lady's ear. And outside in the alley, one of the hippies had bent over and barfed all over the pavement. An usher had come into the booth with the news, and as much as Rance wanted to see that hippie hurling his guts out, he would have had to stop watching the picture and he couldn't do that. For two and half hours he sat there, mesmerized, in the projection booth, watching the movie from way back and high up, looking down on the crowd, some screaming, some covering their eyes, others enraptured, and at the end of it he knew he wanted to spend the rest of his life in the booth. He'd see the world from up here. He'd travel through space and time from up here. He'd watch every human emotion, every laugh, sob, howl, and scream from up here. He'd see it all.

Rance's phone rang, startling him back to himself. It was Marty. "When you getting over here?"

"In a while. I'm still cleaning the popcorn machine."

"I told Claire to do that."

"I sent her home. Told her I'd do it. You really want to pay her for another hour?"

"Goddamnit, Rance, what do I care if she costs me another eight bucks? I got the buyer coming over for the prints!"

"I'll be over soon as I can. Maybe an hour."

"An hour? Jesus."

"The sooner I get off the phone, sooner I'll be there." Rance knew that'd piss him off.

"Hurry up." Marty hung up.

Rance smirked. Shook his head. *The buyer.* Right. Some fucking kid, a nephew of one of Marty's poker buddies, goes off to Hollywood, sells some movie scripts, and is now a film collector. He's rolling in dough and Marty's about to make a killing off this rich kid with money to burn on thirty-five-millimeter prints. The world goes digital and this kid is buying prints. Marty probably tried to sell him the projector to go with them. "If you buy these movies, I'll sell you the projector for cheap." Apparently the kid only wanted the prints.

Rance was hauling up the last of the prints, two cans containing *In Cold Blood,* when the phone rang again. Marty liked that *In Cold Blood* had lots of clean, black-and-white shots of Kansas City. Rance couldn't care less about that. The movie was ponderous and went way too easy on those two killers. And Robert Blake reminded him of his old man. What *was* interesting about *In Cold Blood* was that one of the Finney County sheriff's detectives who'd worked the real-life murder case became a projectionist once he'd retired. Rance met him when he was visiting relatives in Kansas. He'd just walked into the projection booth at the airport drive-in in Hutchinson, and as soon as he started talking projectors with the old guy, all sorts of interesting things came up. They wrote letters back and forth and not long before he passed away he sent a box via special delivery to Rance.

The phone rang again. Rance put down the cans and answered it. Before he could speak, the dull voice on the other end said, "I'm almost there."

"Good, because he's waiting at his house," Rance shot back. "Come up the fire escape in back. I propped the door open."

Rance carried the prints into the booth and when he put them down again he was breathing heavily. It used to be so much easier carrying these things. But then everything used to be easier. He felt tired and worn out. Like this place. He didn't want to see it turned into something else, like what had almost happened to the Brookside and *had* happened to the Fine Arts, now a gutted shit box of a shell used for wedding receptions. He wondered if Marty was doing this just to spite him. Marty was like that. Well, not this time. Rance was lacing up the final reel. *He* was ending this show, not Marty. He was ending Marty too.

He went to the splicing table and opened a drawer under the watchful eyes of Brigitte Bardot, who looked down from the *Contempt* poster on the wall. It was like they were both staring at the drawer. And the snub nose .38 within. This pistol wasn't just called a detective's special, it had actually been one. Etched under the chamber were the words *Finney County S.D.* A gift from the old detective at the drive-in sent special delivery from one "brother of the booth" to another. Rance picked up the gun and it somehow felt heavier than usual, just like the film cans. He heard the squeaking of door hinges and peered out the projection window to see the lanky young man enter through the fire exit. Rance called out, "I'm up here, Ace."

Ace didn't stick around any longer than he had to. The less said between them the better. The last thing Rance gave him was a roll of movie posters, which Ace hadn't expected but welcomed. Rance closed the fire exit after him and imagined what Marty's face would look like when he realized Rance wasn't coming over. Rance wished he could see it for himself but knew that was not to be. He walked back up the aisle a final time and into the lobby.

The platters were spinning in the booth, but the film wasn't going through the projector. Tonight's feature was unspooling onto the floor, celluloid filling the booth like rising floodwaters. Rance backed into the booth, pouring a trail of gasoline across the red-and-gold carpet, emptying the red plastic container. His feet clanged against one of the now empty film cans of Marty's precious collection. The building wouldn't survive the flames, but the cans would remain and Marty would know exactly what they used to contain. They were strewn all over the booth, surrounded by endless strands of shimmering film. Rance unscrewed the lid to another gasoline can and moved through the waist-deep swamp of film. He poured the juice over the splicing bench, doused the projectors, anointed the tendrils of film all around him, and spattered the now bare walls with gas. He wouldn't have dreamed of destroying the posters so he'd passed them on to Ace, who had once been a projectionist himself. Passed on to another "brother of the booth."

It took two matches to get it all going. It would have been nice if one had done the trick. The first match ignited the soaked carpet and shot along from the booth just like it happened in the movies, then branched into two fiery paths: one into the auditorium and the other to the lobby. The fire climbed up the front of the concession counter and engulfed the popcorn machine. Rance moved back into the booth and looked out the small glass window. He watched the line of flame reach the gas-soaked curtain and fan upward over the velvet. The smell of smoke hit his nostrils and he had to fight the urge to just leave the booth, toss another match in, and run away. He had to think about Marty's face and imagine his expression when he got the news that the Rialto was all burned away and his precious films with it.

Then Rance smiled, thinking about Ace and how he'd brought those empty film cans along, just as Rance had instructed. And how he and Rance had loaded Marty's prints into those cans and Ace had taken them away. Marty had hated Ace ever since some coke deal had gone south back in the '80s and Marty wound up empty-handed. He'd held that grudge forever. He was like that.

Rance knew Ace would take good care of Marty's collection. That was comforting. It inspired Rance and he tossed the second match into the mound of film around him. He watched it catch fire and saw the flames consume the walls of the booth. Too bad it wasn't nitrate. This place would really go, then. But it caught fast and the heat rose and hit Rance's face and he thought of humid summers and the welcome cold blast of movie theater AC. Rance clutched the old detective's pistol and without looking closed his eyes and shoved the barrel into his mouth. Then he pulled the trigger and was sure he heard the MGM lion's roar.

CHARLIE PRICE'S LAST SUPPER

BY NADIA PFLAUM

18th and Vine

O n evenings like this, when a thousand pounds of worry pressed down on Charlie Price's shoulders, his gray PT Cruiser seemed to guide itself home. Charlie nearly blinked in surprise when the car nosed into his own driveway, in the empty spot next to the one reserved for his wife's waxed Chrysler 300.

Charlie's anxiety eased when he realized that his wife wouldn't be home for another few hours. It was the first Monday of the month. She'd be at the Black Chamber of Commerce board meeting, milking every ounce of her status as the Spouse of an Important Entrepreneur.

What the board had to gain from her membership, or his, for that matter, was clear as molasses to Charlie. Price's KC Barbecue had a reputation built on sixty-plus years as a local institution, he'd pointed out when his wife dropped the chamber's invitation on his lap.

"It's important to be civilly involved," his wife had said. She used solemn tones, the same ones she'd employed to cajole him into joining St. Matthew's, in the pews of which sat a veritable who's who of prominent black Kansas City.

It wasn't enough simply to attend on Sundays. Never mind that Charlie and his wife had been devotedly secular since their courthouse wedding some twenty-three years prior. No, they had to drop a fortune at Neiman Marcus to cobble together some version of Sunday best, as though the walk from the parking lot's scorching black asphalt to St. Matthew's front doors was a red-carpet, Oscar-night promenade.

Nor was it enough to tithe with a couple bucks from one's billfold. Charlie's wife wanted him to make a big production of unfurling a thick white envelope from his inner coat pocket, passing it to her to place in the wicker basket that came poking into their pew on a wooden stick.

It was all about appearances with her, Charlie grumbled to himself as he shoved open the front door and confronted the stale air of their South Kansas City home. He recalled how his wife had come home from her first Black Chamber board meeting in tears because someone—the wife of some uppity city council so-and-so—had commented on her pearls. "Are they real?" the woman had asked sweetly, and his wife had lied that they were, even though anyone with eyes could plainly see the seam in each plastic bead.

But in recent months, even Charlie had to admit—not aloud, but quietly, to himself—that there was something to be said about maintaining appearances.

When Charles Price Sr., the founder of Price's, died unexpectedly six months ago, Charlie inherited more than his dad's business. Price's was a symbol of Kansas City.

Presidential candidates who came stumping had to be diplomatic in local culinary quarters. They'd run the KC barbecue circuit, sampling the pulled pork and beef-on-bun at Price's and the other historic joints in town. And if asked which meal had been his or her favorite, the candidates invariably declared it a tie.

But a restaurant owner could only ride so far on the dollars of tourists on their obligatory barbecue tours. A flashy, city-subsidized new development had plopped itself squarely in the middle of downtown, and its chain restaurants, with their nationally identical menus, sucked up the trade show–goers and conventioneers with the lust of a fat kid draining the last drops of milk shake from a straw. This new downtown entertainment zone had been constructed posthaste, thanks to a thirty-year tax-abatement deal inked by its out-of-town developers and the city.

And the Black Chamber didn't say a peep. So much for being civicly involved.

For the better part of a century, the *Open* sign at Price's glowed in the window of a low-slung redbrick building on the easternmost section of Kansas City's historic 18th and Vine district. All the action along this strip—if one could call it action after a couple decades of municipal neglect and indifference—happened blocks west, near the Gem Theater, the Negro Leagues Baseball Museum, and the American Jazz Museum. Charlie Price took up the habit of walking the few blocks each morning to the sidewalk where the tour buses stopped and setting up a sandwich board that read, *Don't forget your taste of original KC BBQ at Price's, two blocks east!*

Charlie had to admit that location was the least of his concerns.

While the menu hadn't changed in over fifty years, Price's prices certainly had. They were driven up by the cost of damn near everything, from napkins to soy sauce, sugar to dishwashing detergent. Luckily, Charlie's dad had been wise to purchase land thirty minutes from town, where he placed his lifelong best friend and business partner, Sam, in charge of a small parcel of property to raise hogs and run hickory and cherry logs through a massive wood chipper. Raising one's own pork and buying wood wholesale kept costs down, Charlie knew.

Still, within six months after taking on his late father's operation, Charlie found himself scrimping on some of his signature perks. Gone were the boys in blue Price's jackets who parked cars for patrons who wanted complimentary door-to-door service. An extra cup of cole slaw cost a dollar today, as did refills of red cream soda. The regulars complained, as regulars do. Charlie's dad, Charles Price Sr., had always stressed the importance of rewarding customer loyalty, but whenever Charlie drove past the packed parking lots of chain burger joints on his way to work, he wondered whether loyalty had gone the way of the five-dollar lunch.

Price's wasn't the only barbecue joint that was struggling. Charlie took some solace in the fact that each of the local Big

Three—the three oldest, owner-operated barbecue joints in the city—seemed to suffer equally. It was some comfort, but not much. In their rare get-together, the owners of the Big Three groused about the fickleness of the restaurant industry. Legendary names help, though names sure don't pay the bills.

But the ax had really come down on Charlie a week ago.

That day ended like any other. Charlie walked the perimeter of the restaurant's property, picking up trash and telling loiterers to move along, lobbing his usual threats at the kids who hung out near the bus stop. Charlie took issue with Generation Rap. He didn't like their bomp-bomp-bomp bass, their asses hanging out of sagging pants, the long white T-shirts that made grown men look like toddlers. Charlie assumed they all sold drugs, and in that case, he figured, they ought to be buying more barbecue.

Charlie came back inside as the manager was just switching off the neon signs. He was settling down in the restaurant's office with a fluttering pile of the day's receipts when a man in a red tracksuit and a five-o'clock shadow appeared in the doorway.

C.J. Portello was his name. Said he had been a friend of Charlie's dead father.

"Who wasn't?" Charlie said, not looking up from his desk. "We're closed."

The man in the tracksuit cleared his throat. "We waited six months, out of respect." He stepped into the office to slide a manila folder beneath Charlie's nose. "But now that you've gotten the hang of things, it's time you learned how Charles Sr. really did business."

Charlie picked up the folder by one corner and flipped it open warily.

"Your dad didn't have enough money for a sack of Price's fries when he met my father, James Portello," C.J. said. "All the seed money he used to start this business? That was a loan from us. And for over six decades, that loan has accrued a lot of interest."

Charlie recognized his father's elegant signature on the bottom of a yellowing document in the folder. The document had a lot of fine print, and a lot of zeros.

He stood from his desk abruptly, and just as quickly, the small office filled with the presence of the widest man Charlie had ever seen. The barrel chest came toward him, and towered over him as C.J.'s red tracksuit faded from view. A meaty hand suddenly shot forward and clenched Charlie between the legs, squeezing. The zeros on the printed page swam before Charlie's eyes.

From somewhere that sounded far away, Charlie heard C.J.'s voice: "Now you know the Portello family recipe for pulled pork. Fall behind on your daddy's payments, and we'll repossess what's ours."

After the laugher faded out into the parking lot and he was sure that the visitors were gone, and he no longer felt like throwing up, Charlie got to his feet, stumbled to his car, and drove straight to the farm, and Sam.

Sam was, for all intents and purposes, Charlie's uncle, though his relation to Charles Sr. wasn't through blood. The men knew each other from "the block," 38th and Forest, and that's where they had reunited after each was medically discharged from Vietnam, six months apart.

When they went into the barbecue business together, Charles Sr. wore the suits and did the glad-handing and ribbon-cutting. Meanwhile, Sam wore muddy overalls, kept the hogs fed, and when it was time, slaughtered them.

Charlie parked his PT Cruiser in the grass and followed an extension cord that snaked from Sam's bare-bones house and across the weed-specked dirt, out to the woodshed, which sat beside the gate to the hog pen. At the terminus of the cord, Charlie found an oscillating fan, a laptop, and Sam, his face bathed in the screen's green glow.

Charlie thrust the folder from Portello between Sam's nose and the laptop screen.

"What do you know about this?" Charlie demanded.

Sam took the folder and opened it, leaning back slowly on the stepladder he was using as a stool. He squinted. His white-flecked eyebrows raised. "I'll be damned," he muttered.

Charlie leaned against a wall full of tools and rubbed his forehead with both hands.

"Looks like your father was paying the Portellos $1,000 a month toward their $250,000 investment," Sam went on. "But at the rate of interest these greaseballs set, he never made a dent."

Charlie paced back and forth in the shed. "Nobody can know about this," he said. "I can barely make payroll. I can't pay these guys. They're going to kill me and take Price's and turn it into a spaghetti factory."

In the months since Charles Sr. died, Charlie had leaned on Sam heavily. The older man always seemed to have the answers. But tonight was different.

"I suppose you'll have to find a way," is all Sam said.

The following night, after another long day slinging meat—or, more accurately, watching his employees sling meat—Charlie came home again to a dark house. Charlie's wife, he knew, was at her weekly bible study. He emptied the bulging pockets of his work pants—the janitor-sized key ring, his cell phone, a couple packets of wet naps—and plunked it all on the dining room table before settling on the couch and turning on the TV.

On the local news, a reporter stood in front of a ramshackle East Kansas City house whose front lawn was crisscrossed with yellow tape. Another homicide. Charlie sighed. Was it really necessary for the reporters to broadcast live in front of the scene, as aunties and cousins wailed in the background? Promising updates, the broadcast mercifully segued into commercials.

That's when Charlie saw it.

"*THIS SATURDAY NIGHT*," the commercial boomed, as a relentless bassline made Charlie scramble for the volume button, "Kansas City's own MAJOR PLAYER RECORDS drops the album of the summer on you, from their HOTTEST RECORDING ARTIST YET."

All at once, the screen was overtaken by a pair of lips. A finger came into the frame, hushing the lips. On the finger was a gold ring. And on the ring, nine flawless diamonds formed a glittering *P*.

"Y'all ain't seen nothin' till you see this," drawled the owner of that ring, the man himself, Major Player.

As the commercial blared the whats and wheres of the concert, Charlie grabbed a pen from an end table and scribbled a note to himself on the back of a packet of wet naps.

The next day at the restaurant, Charlie made his way through the kitchen's swinging aluminum doors. He found Marcus, the twenty-five-year-old busboy, filling up a soapy pail of mop water by the back door.

"What's the deal with Major Player?" Charlie asked the kid.

Marcus looked up. "Huh?"

Charlie paused, suddenly self-conscious.

Marcus had been one of his father's last hires before he died. Charles Price Sr. had marveled aloud over the young man's promise and potential. Charlie didn't understand how anyone, at twenty-five, could be satisfied with being a busboy. Guess some guys just didn't aspire to much.

"I mean, who is Major Player?" Charlie said. "What's his story?"

Marcus dunked his mop in the suds thoughtfully. "Player's like the godfather," he said. "You want to be a rapper, you pretty much gotta go through him."

"You know him?" Charlie wanted to know.

A smile crept across Marcus's lips. "I seen him around."

"Where'd he get the kind of money he's flashing around on TV?"

Marcus shrugged. "They say he use the music as a front for drug money. Streets talk, but half of it's bullshit."

"More like three-fourths," Charlie said, and grinned. He looked down at the bucket. "Don't let me hold you up." He took two steps toward the back door, then swiveled around again. "If someone wanted to find Major Player," Charlie asked, "where'd they go looking?"

"If I was you," Marcus said, stabbing at the suds with the mop, "I'd try 9th Wonder."

Fifteen minutes later, Charlie was staring up at 9th Wonder's green neon sign, the letters reflected in reverse off the lenses of his glasses. The wood-shingled building stood alone on a block where other structures sagged under the weight of time, neglect, and rot, ultimately succumbing to the city's bulldozers. This place stood impervious to the surrounding decay, its service to vice like an invisible force field. Inside, 9th Wonder was one part head shop, one part adult video emporium, and one part urban record store.

Charlie pushed through the jangling door whose glass was completely papered over with concert posters and triple-X handbills. He propelled himself past shelves jammed with glass bongs, walking straight ahead to the front counter. At its zenith stood a woman with a wrist-thick, blue-black ponytail and press-on nails like neon daggers.

The clerk peered down with practiced disinterest. She raised one eyebrow, skinny as a spider's leg. It seemed to indicate that Charlie should speak first.

"I'm here to see Mr., uh, Player," Charlie said.

Charlie got the feeling that the clerk knew a thousand different ways to say no. Before she had a chance to choose one, he blurted, "I have a business proposition for him."

The clerk unfurled a long, bony finger. Its day-glo nail pointed in the direction of a set of emerald curtains. Charlie thanked her and plunged into the green velvet darkness.

On the other side of the curtain, three men sat at a round card table in a cigar-smoke haze, a heap of money between them. At Charlie's entrance, two of the men scraped their chairs back and stood. Both had fists the size of hams.

"Relax, fellas," the still-seated man said. Charlie heard the unmistakable crack of a gun being cocked. "Can we help you?"

Charlie swallowed. "I'm not sure I'm in the right place, but my name is Charlie Price and I came to find Major Player."

"You found him," the owner of the voice said, leaning forward, into the light. "Did you say Charlie Price?"

"Yes." Charlie could hear his heart beating in his ears.

"Man, get over here!" Major Player said, pushing back his chair with a screech. The rap mogul danced around the card table to throw his arms around him. Charlie patted the man's back awkwardly. Had he been wearing a tie, Major Player's head would be level with the knot.

"It is a pleasure to be in the presence of the man responsible for the finest burnt ends in Killa City, yahdidamean?" Player said, gesturing for Charlie to take a seat at the table. Charlie reached for the back of a chair, his eyes bouncing between Player's two thick-necked bookends.

"Mind if we had some privacy?" Charlie asked Player.

With a wave of one sparkly hand, Player dismissed his goons. When the green curtain's swishing ceased, Charlie took a deep breath and began: "I came to ask you what you'd do if you were me." He flourished Portello's folder. As he passed it to Player, he was embarrassed to notice the wet spots on the paper from his sweaty palms.

Player reached under his XXL T-shirt and pulled out a pair of reading glasses. His lips moved as he scanned the page. After several moments, he slammed the glasses down.

"WHAT? Aw, hell naw. Them fake-Gucci-ass wannabe Corleones ain't gonna hustle a BLACK business owner in MY city." Beads of sweat popped out around Player's collar as he grew more heated. "Nobody does you like this, Charlie Price, yahdidamean?"

"Right. Wait, what?" Charlie said. There was no telling where this was going, but something about it felt right.

"Here's what I'm fittin' to do for YOU," Player continued, his voice tremulous like a Pentecostal preacher about to produce a snake. "I'ma work this out with the Eye-talians. This money ain't nothin' to me."

Charlie didn't know what to say. "How will I repay you?" he asked.

"Oh, you'll repay me, believe that," Player replied, winking. "But who'd you rather owe, some Louisville-Slugger, kneecap-bustin' Eye-talian, or your ol' friend Major Player?"

Charlie got up from his chair, botched a fist bump with the mogul's outstretched knuckles, and floundered back through the green curtain.

"And don't ever say Major Player don't look out for you, fam," Player called after him.

That night, he took his wife out for dinner. "Anyplace you want, dear," he told her. "Just not barbecue."

When Charlie strolled into Price's the following evening, it was a couple hours after the dinner rush. An unfamiliar black Escalade was parked in the lot next to Marcus's Caprice.

Inside, there was more commotion than usual. Charlie soon saw why: Major Player was standing on the bar, directing his twin goons, who each held an end of a tape measure.

"See, if we take out these two booths and raise the floor a foot, this here becomes a stage, with a pole right here," he was saying to the goons, and to Marcus, who stood behind the bar, nodding.

Charlie waited in the doorway until he was noticed.

"My man," Player said, hopping off the bar and striding over, fist poised for a bump.

Charlie ignored the fist. "What's all this?"

"Well, I been thinking," Player said. "I've always wanted to get into the restaurant business. And last night, I saw our boy Portello and squared you with him, whoop-de-whoop. So I figure now I'm a partner. And hoo-wee, we got some updating to do in this mu'fucka."

Player grabbed the first server who passed by the wrist. "See here—what's your name, gorgeous?" he asked.

"Shanay," she answered shyly.

"We gotta sexify this," Player said, spinning her like a two-stepper. "This buttoned-up-collared-shirt business, this don't do nothin' for your figure, baby. We need to be showing off more of this." He traced the curves of Shanay's backside, and she giggled. "Some little shorts, and something low-cut on top. Give the people something extra on they lunch hour."

Player released the girl's wrist and paced slowly in front of the bar. "We gotta do something about the music," he said. The diamond *P* in his ring sparkled as he placed his index finger behind one ear. "This Charlie Parker shit has got to go. I don't know if this was the ol' man's taste," he went on, looking to the black-and-white photo of Charlie Sr. standing proudly in front of the Price's sign, which had hung behind the bar for as long as Charlie could remember. "But we need to get the 808s bumping. This could be a hoppin' after-hours spot. Twelve bucks a shot of Hennessy, boy, we'll need an armored truck every night when we leave, yahdidamean?"

Suddenly, Charlie needed some air. He gave Player a weak smile. "I got a few calls to make. Excuse me," he said, and retreated through the kitchen doors.

Charlie closed the door to the business office and phoned Sam, who answered after a dozen rings.

"Sam, this is bad," Charlie whispered. His voice sounded panicky and he didn't care. "Major Player—he's a rapper, or something—he bought the debt from Portello. But now he wants to be a partner in Price's. He wants to change everything, make this place some sort of—rap clubhouse, or something." He gasped for breath. "My dad will roll in his grave. My wife will have a stroke."

Sam was silent for a moment. Then he said, "Well, if he wants to be a partner, invite him up to the farm. We can explain things to him so he understands."

Charlie exhaled heavily. "You're always right, Sam. I hope you're right now."

For the next hour, Charlie cleared his head by playing solitaire on the office computer. When things seemed sufficiently quiet on the other side of the door, he headed to the kitchen. Inside the walk-in freezer, he chose a hunk of roast beef the size of his head, pulled back the plastic, and prepared to cut himself a snack's worth on the meat slicer. As the blade started whirring, Charlie heard the *snik-snik* sounds of metal against metal. He cut the motor. The circular blade looked painfully ragged. Ignoring the growling in his stomach, Charlie engrossed himself in the task of breaking down the slicer to free the blade for sharpening.

Minutes later, the aluminum double doors of the kitchen burst open, and there stood Major Player, teetering like a man on a dinghy. A bottle of Hennessy dangled from the fingers of one hand, the last inch of amber liquid sloshing against the glass.

"I hada ideal," Player said. "I invited the whooole crew from the label to come out and celebrate my new business vulture."

Charlie mumbled something, not making eye contact.

Player steadied himself and regarded Charlie with bloodshot eyes. "I get this vibe from you, Charlie," the rapper slurred. "I don't mean no disrespect, but I'm not sure yerr bein' so receptical to my ideals."

Charlie whirled around, preparing the words in his head. *Nah, Player*, he planned to say. *This place is my legacy. We'll have to find some other way to settle this debt.*

The drunk man lurched forward, trying to throw a chummy arm around Charlie's shoulders. Charlie took a step and caught Player under the arms as he toppled over. The Hennessy bottle crashed on the concrete floor.

"Put it on my tab," Player grinned.

Something warm and wet slid down Charlie's arm. He pulled back. The meat slicer's blade, still in his grip, dripped with blood.

Player stared at the object in Charlie's hand, then reached up and felt the slit in the armpit of his T-shirt. He pulled down on the fabric, tearing it wider, to reveal a gash that spurted in time with his heartbeat.

"The fuck . . ." Player said, pitching forward.

Charlie set the bloody blade on the counter and ran for the telephone in his office. When he reached the doorway, he stopped and looked back to the kitchen. A streak of blood was making its way from Player's shuddering body to the drain in the center of the floor.

Charlie walked slowly back into the kitchen. He stepped gingerly over the trail of blood, tiptoed past Player, whose body now lay still, and peered out the cloudy window in the back door. The black Escalade sat, still parked, but Charlie could see that the driver's-side window was open. One of Player's goons was at the wheel, his head lolled back against the headrest.

Charlie hit the unlock button on his key at the same time as he forced the door open. He darted on the tips of his toes to his PT Cruiser, got in, started the engine, and backed it from his parking space up to Price's back door. He cut the engine and got back out, slamming the door hard. The goon's head jerked up at the sound.

"Hey, man," Charlie said, feigning calm. "What you still doin' here?"

The goon grunted. "Waitin' on Player," he replied, rubbing his eyes.

"Man, Player left," Charlie said. "He was pretty gone, you know, off that Hennessy." He laughed. "Didn't want to wake you, so I took him home."

The goon blinked. "Aiight," he said finally, turning the key in the Escalade.

Charlie waved at the diminishing taillights before heading back inside.

Once the back door shut, Charlie focused. He unfurled four black trash bags. He straddled Player's still-warm body and shimmied a bag under the man's Chuck Taylors, all the way to his waist.

He shoved Player's head and shoulders into another bag. Then he threw an additional bag over each for good measure, and cinched all four bags at the dead rapper's waist with the cotton string used for cooking roasts. He gathered the entire, unwieldy mass up in his arms and hauled it out the back door.

The PT Cruiser's trunk was roomy. Slamming the trunk shut, Charlie heaved a sigh and looked around. At the bus stop twenty yards away, a bum hiccupped, then saluted. Charlie hesitated, then saluted in return before going back inside.

A white bucket was the cooking staff's solution for collecting the water that leaked from the bar's soda fountain. Charlie grabbed it and heaved its contents across the kitchen's concrete floor. Pink water swirled around the drain.

Charlie rinsed the bloody slicer blade in the dish sink and stuck it on a handful of clean rags in the drying rack. He wiped up the spatters of blood from the countertops and, as an afterthought, the tops of his own shoes.

Then Charlie turned off all the lights, locked the doors, and peeled out in the PT Cruiser, spraying gravel. The bum at the bus stop burped and waved.

Charlie called Sam from his cell phone five minutes from the farm. It was two o'clock in the morning. Sam answered after seven rings. He was waiting outside when Charlie pulled up.

"Sarge," Sam said to Charlie as soon as he opened the door.

Charlie turned off the car but left the headlights on. Wordlessly, Sam and Charlie heaved Major Player's plastic-bound carcass from the trunk to the edge of Sarge's section of pen.

Sarge, the boar that had fathered Price's latest passel of pork, was a ravenous, foul-tempered beast that had to be separated from his progeny, lest he eat the baby swine.

Sam mopped sweat from his eyes. He yanked the cotton string, pulled away the trash bags, and eyed the remains. Leaning down, he grabbed one of Player's bloodstained hands and began to yank.

"What are you doing?" Charlie hissed, looking away.

"Here," Sam said, tossing him something that glinted in the car's headlights. Charlie missed, and felt around in the moist weeds at his feet until he came up with something small, gold, and glittering. He held it in the headlight's beam. The ring, with its diamond *P*, spat light in his eyes. He shoved it down deep in his pocket and looked to Sam.

"Let's go," Sam said, and grabbed the dead man's ankles. Charlie took the wrists. They pitched forward and back, until the swing had momentum enough for Player's dead weight to clear the five-foot wood fence posts. The body hit on Sarge's side of the pen with a sloppy thud.

Sam and Charlie eyed each other in the settling dust. After a moment, there was the sound of rustling hay, and snorting, and then the sound of teeth splitting bone.

Charlie doubled over and dry heaved. Sam ignored him, moved to the PT Cruiser, and peered into the trunk.

"You're gonna want to get this clean," he said.

Charlie rolled his eyes. "Thank you, Sam."

"Leave it here," Sam said, cupping his hands for Charlie's keys and tossing another set in return. "Take the Ford."

Charlie missed again, but felt around in the grass for the keys to Sam's 1960 F100 Ford truck. When he looked up, he saw Sam's back disappearing into the darkness toward the woodshed. "Hey," said Charlie.

Sam turned, made a shooing motion with both hands, and kept walking.

The F100 backfired maddeningly all the way home on I-70. It forced Charlie to drive the speed limit. It was 3:45 by the time he pulled into his driveway.

Charlie stripped off his clothes in the basement and shoved them into the washing machine, switching the setting to hot. In the blackness, he crawled into bed next to his snoring wife and stared at the ceiling until the room filled with light.

* * *

The disappearance of Major Player made the news after two days. On the third day, Charlie called Sam to say that he thought it was time for Sarge to give the ultimate sacrifice to Price's. Sam delivered the butcher-paper-wrapped cuts of meat to the restaurant in Charlie's freshly detailed PT Cruiser.

And on the seventh day, Charlie prepared to host Major Player's entourage, despite the absence of the rap mogul himself.

That morning, as he left the house, Charlie told his wife that she ought to stop by Price's that evening. He'd learned, years ago, the consequences of leaving her out of a restaurant celebration. "Wear something special," he told her with a wink.

That day, Charlie had the kitchen humming. Generous portions of Sarge, incarnate in dollops of pulled pork atop buttery biscuits, appeared with a flourish on plates. Marcus stopped and greeted each table as guests were seated. Charlie caught himself looking twice at guys dressed Major Player–style in long white tees.

Charlie was directing the proportioning of cole slaw on plates when he sensed that things had become ominously quiet on the restaurant floor. He exited the kitchen's swinging doors to see a man holding a badge in the doorway. Marcus the busboy looked to Charlie helplessly.

"Ladies and gentlemen," the cop said loudly, "I'm Detective Phillips, as some of you may know."

The occupants of several of the tables grew visibly uncomfortable.

"As many of you also know, an individual who goes by the name of Major Player has been missing for over a week," Detective Phillips went on. "I am all too familiar with the culture that says that you ought not cooperate with authorities like myself."

The detective held some business cards aloft, then placed them by the racks of weekly papers near the entrance. "This Major Player is, I understand, a friend and associate to many of you, so I'm simply placing a stack of my cards here by the door for anyone who is concerned for his welfare and wishes to contact me at a later date."

The detective was in the midst of his parting words when the front doors opened behind him. Charlie recognized the silhouette of his wife in a figure-hugging gray dress as she squeezed past the cop and scanned the restaurant floor.

Charlie hurried toward her, untying the apron he wore over his clothes. "Paulette!" he greeted warmly, kissing her on both cheeks. "We, too, are deeply concerned for Mr. Player and his family," he said over his shoulder to the detective, guiding his wife toward an empty table.

"Hold on, Mr. Price," the detective said, with a hand on Charlie's shoulder. "I don't believe we've met."

Charlie whirled around with his best how-do-you-do face. He placed a hand on his wife's back to present her the way she'd taught him the night that he'd accompanied her to her first formal Chamber event. And as he did so, he spotted a gleam around her neck. Paulette had strung Major Player's diamond ring on a chain and was wearing it as a necklace

The detective saw the ring at precisely the same moment. "Why, hello," he said. "Mrs. Price, I assume? Now where did you get that lovely piece of jewelry around your neck?"

Charlie's wife beamed. "You know, I was just doing the laundry this morning, and earlier, Charlie had told me to dress up tonight for some big affair. And wouldn't you know, he left this ring in his pants pocket for me to find?"

"I see," Detective Phillips said, with exaggerated interest. "And is that a *P* written on that ring, in diamonds?"

Paulette smiled demurely. "Why, yes."

"Can I have a moment in private?" The detective's hand snaked up to grip Charlie's arm. "If you'll excuse us, ma'am."

Sam emerged from where he'd been helping in the kitchen to see the detective guide Charlie through the front door. Sam's eyes met Marcus's, and the busboy wandered over.

"Seems like," Sam whispered in the busboy's ear, "Charles Sr.'s predictions are coming to pass."

And Marcus nodded.

THE PENDERGAST MUSKET

BY PHONG NGUYEN

West Bottoms

Jim Pendergast, 1882

After I took in all that money from the races, Papa Pendergast told me a joke I won't soon forget.

A rich man walks into a saloon and says, "I read in the news today that Andrew Carnegie gave a hundred thousand dollars to the poor. I've had some good fortune in my day, and I too would like to devote my life to philanthropy. Can you tell me where I can find the poor?" So the drunkard to his right chimes up and says, "Well, sir, I've been laid off from my job at the factory since last Tuesday and my back hurts so bad from the fifteen years I worked there I can hardly take another job. I'm mighty hard up and I wouldn't mind an act of grace whether it comes from the Lord or His messengers on earth." So with a tear in his eye and a kind word, the rich man gives him a hundred dollars.

Hearing this, the drunkard to his left leans over and says, "Lord knows that no man can measure his suffering against another's, but I can tell you that I've never known what it's like to make a decent day's wages. I was orphaned by the war and raised on a railroad car, never had a bed of my own and grew up so sickly nobody'd employ me. Last week I got my first real job, at the factory, and wouldn't you know it but before I get my first bank note, they up and fire me last Wednesday." With a consoling look, the rich man reaches into his breast pocket and pulls out another hundred, pressing it into the drunkard's palm with a handshake.

Pretty soon all the drunkards are clamoring around and telling him stories, each one surpassing the last in the details of their poverty and the depth of their suffering, but pretty soon he starts to notice a recurring trend in all their stories. It appears that every one of them has been fired from a local factory last week. After giving away every hundred-dollar bill that he owns, the rich man turns red-faced with anger, imagining the soulless tycoon who bankrupted this whole town.

Turning to the bartender, the rich man says, "I have done all that I possibly can within my means, and now I will go make my fortune again, so I can do more good works for the poor. But before I go, may I ask you, who is this terrible tyrant who hires men at the factory, works them to death, then puts them out on the street when nothing is left of them but tales of woe?"

Looking blankly at the rich man, the bartender says, "Why, sir, I thought you already knew. It's Andrew Carnegie!"

I've spent too much time over the years looking for a moral. *Money will ruin your soul. Never trust a rich man.* But I figure the keystone is this: *If you get rich, resist the temptation to give to the poor, because they'll have it all, and pretty soon you'll be the poor.*

After some years I figured out that Papa meant it as a sort of strategy, a way of living in the harsh world of business, which he knew I was fixing to enter: *If you're the richest man in the world, all you have to do is give away a little; in trying to emulate you, your competition will impoverish themselves.*

But at the age of twenty-two, this is all I heard: "Be a saloon keeper, son, and you'll learn everybody's secrets."

It's six a.m., the dog's hour, when I unlock the doors and let the first customers in. By opening time I've already had the night cops coming off their beat, playing one last game of rummy and shooting fistfuls of whiskey so they'll have something to sleep off, and one salesman who sets up at the bar and keeps looking at the door after every sip, trying to muster the strength to kick back the stool and get out—an Irishman named Whelan, I let him in early because he's more than just a regular; he's like furniture now.

Besides, I take pride in the way my establishment welcomes every soul, provides a second home to all of the lost, and Whelan is the most lost sonuvabitch I've ever seen.

Right away Rob Toke comes in with an antique musket he wants to sell, to keep him in drink for another week. His short hair is brushed back, making it stick up part of the way like stepped-on grass. He's got lady hips and a torso that can't seem to keep any weight, a sharp nose and a way of raising his eyebrows when he talks that makes him look surprised by his own words. I'm just the opposite, I suppose: heavy around the middle, slim in the legs, and as excitable as an Indian chief.

"Ain't she a beauty?" he says, cradling the musket like a baby. He places it down on the wood grain by the cask ale.

Leaning over it so I can smell the gunpowder, I shrug. "It's not from the war, I'll tell you that much."

"Not the war between the states, my friend," he says, running his fingers along the Dutch lock, a hundred-year-old span of iron, admirably worn. "The War of Independence. It belonged to my great-grandpa."

Seeing as he hasn't put a musket ball through me, I can only assume he brought it in hoping to sell it off. "Does this look like a pawnshop to you, Toke?"

"Come on, Jim," he says. "It's just a gift. I figure since my dad's passed, it's better to get rid of all the old stuff." He fidgets, looks away from the gun, scans the room, lingering on the tap. I've always liked Toke, but no man ever wore his weaknesses so openly as him.

"But if you were interested, I'd take a week of drinks in trade."

I stare at him a long time. I mean a long time. "Take your treasure and bury it, Toke. In my place, no good man ever goes thirsty."

He brushes back his prickly hair, mutters his thanks, and waits a full forty seconds before filling his glass.

John, Michael, even Hannah, or for that matter any of my brothers or sisters, have a job waiting for them at The Climax—which I named for the horse on whom I won my fortune—if they find themselves out of work, but only Tom actually shows up every day to clean the place the way a worker is supposed to. And the boy is all of ten. Trouble is he's starting to talk like a saloon regular, and John has reported as much to our mother.

"You teetotaling sonuvabitch," Tom says to John that afternoon. Then he turns to me like he's tattling to Mom. "As soon as John showed up last night he started cutting customers off at three drinks."

John makes a production of polishing the counter, ignoring the wily runt in front of him. "This way of life—the kind of business you run—isn't long for this world," he says, dropping his Christian wisdom on the saloon floor like rose petals.

"Nothing is, Johnny," I say, dropping my saloon wisdom on him like a horse pile. John has wet-looking hair that falls down on his broad forehead in pointy strands, and manly features that stand in contrast to the bruised expressions he often wears. He could have been on the rugby team at college. Tom's hair is similarly straight, but it moves away from the front of his head like it's afraid to get in the way of his little bulldog face.

"Close up, will you?" I say to John as Tom and I make for the door. "And keep the tap flowing until the midnight hour. We're gonna get the hell out of the Bottoms tonight."

Tom and I have always been Folly Theater faithfuls. They mean to keep a body entertained, and weekdays or weekends I've never had to suffer through a miserable opera or melodrama or traveling lecture. They get the best comics, jugglers, hypnotists, magicians, and quick-drawers on the circuit every time. Last week it was a plate spinner who kept up to eight pieces of fine china going at once; tonight it's a more elevating form of relaxation: a traveling show, the wonders of the wizard of Menlo Park. Mr. Edison won't be making an appearance himself, of course, but two of his assistants, trained in the operation of his phonographic and incandescent machines, will be.

The ushers at the Folly walk the aisles and pass around printed cards from silver trays, while wearing gloves; Tom rolls his eyes at me, and I mutter a plea to the Lord that the Folly isn't going swanky. As it turns out, written on the cards are merely reminders not to smoke in the theater, as the equipment being used today is sensitive, and combustible. We sink in our chairs, Tom more than I, and light our pipes anyway.

A gentleman in a mustache and a white suit walks through the parted curtains and down the center of the stage, to faint applause, while behind him an assistant—a long-legged lady—wheels a table full of contraptions out into the middle. For her, the audience gives a more stirring welcome, with some hoots and howls thrown into the mix.

Though he looks convincingly foreign, the man's speech betrays his Midwestern origins. Cynically, I conclude that he's not even an inventor's assistant from New Jersey, but a Chicagoan who purchased some sophisticated new equipment, trained himself to use it, and now travels week-long tours with his pretty young wife to satellite cities like St. Paul, Indianapolis, and Detroit, where they stay at the Savoy and the Ritz, getting royal treatment just for throwing around Edison's name.

"Men and women of Kansas City, today you are going to see—and hear—some of the most revolutionary science that man has ever devised. So prepare yourselves for the impossible."

First they set up the phonograph. A baritone voice bellows in operatic Italian, from the very walls it seems, followed by a procession of voices and a swelling music. I guess the Folly is going swanky after all. At first I think that they must have a chorus and band hidden beneath the stage, the way that, I'm told, magicians will hide doves and rabbits in cages underneath the planks of wood; but then he shuts off the machine, and all that's left is the ghost of an echo.

Then, while the mustachioed gentleman is doing his demonstration of incandescence, one of the ushers takes the stage and whispers in the ear of his assistant. After the next bout of applause the mustache steps forward and says, "The proprietors of the Folly Theater have asked me to make a public announcement. During yesterday's Wild West show, a valuable and rare Revolutionary War musket was stolen off the back of Winnifred the sharpshooter's wagon trailer. Anyone with information leading to the return of the firearm and the arrest of the man who stole it will receive a considerable reward. Now, on with the show!"

I don't stand up and leave the theater abruptly because to do so right after such an announcement would implicate me; but I am sorely tempted. I need to find and warn Toke, then I need to strangle the bastard for trying to unload his ill-gotten gains on me.

The next day, as we get ready to open, I gather the family together—by blood and by labor—and we sit around quiet, waiting for Winston, who used to be a roughneck with me in the ironworking days before The Climax, and who now serves as the doorkeeper. Finally Winston lumbers in and pulls back a chair. Winston's sort is an indispensable friend when you live and work in the Bottoms. I lead off: "I have something to say. Not one of you is gonna talk to the law today or any day. Even if they're offering a hundred dollars for information about that gun. It don't matter. If they ask, *Have you seen a man walking around with a Revolutionary War musket in his arms?* you just laugh in their faces. They'll get used to it. Understand?"

"You ain't gonna back the bastard, are you?" Tom says. "You might as good get hauled off to jail."

"Shut your bone box, Tom. This ain't your fight," I reply.

"I knew this business would bite you back," says John automatically, and even he seems to sense that his sanctimonious posture has gone, perhaps, too far. Folks are staring at the two of us, and Winston lifts his eyebrow.

Tom starts to pipe up, but I show him a finger. "Take whatever you were about to say and pocket it, Tommy." Then I turn to John. "You can condemn my immortal soul to your heart's content, Johnny," I tell him, "but say nothing to the law about the musket."

At that, we all stand up, ready to get to work. Just then Whelan, who we hardly noticed sitting on the stool at the bar's end, stands up, sober as a churchwoman, and says, "I seen that boy Toke with the same one."

It's such a shock to see him on his feet, that between registering the quick pace of his speech and taking in the size of him, we're all of us still and silent as the shadows of houses.

"TJ, Mike, John, Gil, Winston, go do the books," I say, and the five men—a couple of them just boys—move to the back room and give us the floor of the saloon.

Standing off with Irish, I notice for the first time that he's a hairline above my six feet. "What're you playing at, Whelan?"

"I'm not playing at all, you old rusty guts. When you put down a month's wages on a longshot and the horse came in first place, Jim, that was your day." He breathes on his hands as though it's cold in the saloon. His first day without firewater in so many years, his body doesn't know how to make its own warmth. "Today I heard somebody'd pay a hundred dollars for a piece of information that I happen to know, so today is my day."

"Listen good, peckerwood. You didn't hear what you think you heard," I say. But damned Whelan has heard me bark before.

"I'm gonna walk out of that door, and I'm gonna go to the authorities. It's up to you whether you want to stand in my way."

I step aside.

"Go to the police. I hope you do. They'll come in here and say, *Jim, your regular Whelan said he saw the musket offered you by a boy by the name of Toke.* And I'll say, *Sir, that Whelan couldn't see a hole in a ladder,* and that'll be the end of it." I grab the broom, sweep the floor by the entrance, and give him a butler's bow.

"Winston!" I call out, and the big man steps through the door frame, nearly filling it with his bulk. "Bounce him."

Winston steps in the room, followed by Tom, and the two of them crowd Whelan out the door. By the morning street among the rushers, Winston says, "I just wish I could see the cops' faces when the lousiest drunk in Kansas City walks into their station with his tail down and his face busted up from a bar brawl." The glass doors swing closed, and I can see them, but barely hear them talk.

Whelan touches his cheek, as though expecting to find something there, and says, "But my face is—"

It's just then that Winston gives him a nose-ender, laying him out on the street.

Tom walks back in the saloon and picks up the broom that I set against the jamb. Then he steps back out holding it halfway down like a baseball club.

I find Toke on the banks of the Missouri, still skulking around the Bottoms, with the stolen musket hidden in a rolled quilt. I'm just glad he didn't wash up there like a dead fish.

"The word downtown is you stole that musket," I say matter-of-factly.

"I left him a coin," he responds with a laugh that he couldn't help even if he were sober. Seeing how I'm not laughing, he straightens up good and quick. "Jimmy, you gotta understand. He just left it out there in the back alley. If I didn't take it, someone else would've."

"But you tried to shed your burden onto me," I say.

Toke blinks maybe a hundred times.

"It's okay, Toke. I've already seen one man get a hiding today. Besides, you're a bully trap."

He smiles like a schoolboy, then corrects himself. "Whelan, was it? The man?"

"Don't worry who. Man is a loyal creature by nature, and I'm no different. The kind I know that don't generally follow that line are beneath being called men."

With that we started walking the seven blocks to The Climax. We went silently, cutting through an uncontrollably red Missouri dusk. At the door, I turned to Toke and shook his hand, then lit my pipe.

"You know, Whelan said my lucky break came on the day Climax won the big race. But he's wrong about that. Someday I'll be called for an even higher purpose, and when I am, I'll need a big family. Are you my family, Toke?"

He nods vigorously, his eyebrows shouting their consent.

"What are we gonna do now?" he asks.

"There ain't but the one solution," I say. "Gimme the musket."

Toke doesn't hesitate, doesn't fret with worry over what ills might befall me for taking on his burdens.

After the boy leaves, and the windows have gone dark as scotch ale, I drag one of the barstools behind the counter, climb up so my boots pinch on the upholstery, and in the plain view of thirty men, mount the old musket above the mirror backing. As if to say, I'd do the same for any of you. As though to dare any stranger who walks through the doors of The Climax to just try and boast of their own kindnesses.

ABOUT THE CONTRIBUTORS

Paul Andrews

MITCH BRIAN cocreated and wrote episodes for *Batman: The Animated Series* and cowrote the NBC miniseries *The '70s.* He has written screenplays for producers and directors including Chris Columbus, Oliver Stone, Geena Davis, James Ellroy, and Robert Schwentke. His plays are published by Dramatic Publishing and have been produced worldwide. He teaches screenwriting and film studies at the University of Missouri—Kansas City.

David Remley

CATHERINE BROWDER is a Kansas City–based fiction writer and playwright, with two story collections published: *The Clay That Breathes* and *Secret Lives.* Her plays have been produced regionally and in New York, and her awards include fellowships from the NEA and the Missouri Arts Council. She teaches in the creative writing program at the University of Missouri, Kansas City, and is advisory editor for *New Letters.*

Katie Cramer Eck

MATTHEW ECK was recently recognized as one of the National Book Foundation's "5 under 35" writers to watch. His novel *The Farther Shore* won the Milkweed National Fiction Prize and was a Barnes and Noble Discover Great New Writers selection. The novel has been translated into German and Norwegian. He is a professor of creative writing and literature at the University of Central Missouri, where he is also a fiction editor for *Pleiades.*

Dave Anderson

J. MALCOLM GARCIA is the author of *The Khaarijee: A Chronicle of Friendship and War in Kabul* (Beacon, 2009), and *Riding through Katrina with the Red Baron's Ghost* (Kindle Edition, 2010). His articles have been featured in *Best American Travel Writing* and *Best American Nonrequired Reading.*

Jennifer Lutz-Bauer

JOHN LUTZ is the author of more than forty novels, including *SWF Seeks Same, The Ex, Mister X,* and two private-eye series, one set in St. Louis, the other in Florida. He's a past president of the Mystery Writers of America and the Private Eye Writers of America, and has won awards from those organizations and others. He lives in St. Louis and Sarasota, Florida.

Sarah Nguyen

PHONG NGUYEN'S first collection of short stories, *Memory Sickness*, won the 2010 Elixir Press Fiction Award; his stories have appeared in numerous literary magazines, including *Agni, Beloit Fiction Journal, Boulevard, Florida Review, Iowa Review, Massachusetts Review, New Ohio Review, Meridian,* and *Portland Review*. Formerly editor of *Cream City Review,* he currently serves as editor of *Pleiades,* and is an associate professor of fiction at the University of Central Missouri.

Carol Zastoupil

STEVE PAUL has worked at the *Kansas City Star* since 1975. As senior writer and arts editor, he writes about music, books, architecture, food, and other subjects. His book *Architecture A to Z: An Elemental, Alphabetical Guide to Kansas City's Built Environment* was published in 2011. He is coeditor of *War + Ink,* a forthcoming collection of essays on Ernest Hemingway, and a former director of the National Book Critics Circle.

Walt Whitaker

NADIA PFLAUM is a freelance writer and legal investigator in Kansas City. Her nonfiction work has been published in Kansas City's alt-weekly, *The Pitch,* on *Salon,* and in *Best Music Writing 2008.*

Phil Shafer

NANCY PICKARD is the author of eighteen popular and critically acclaimed novels, including the Jenny Cain and Marie Lightfoot mystery series. She is a four-time Edgar Award finalist and has won the Agatha, Anthony, Macavity, Barry, and Shamus awards. Pickard is a founding member and former president of Sisters in Crime.

Mary Y. Hallab

KEVIN PRUFER is the author of numerous critically acclaimed books of poetry. His mysteries appear in *Alfred Hitchcock's Mystery Magazine, Crimewave,* and elsewhere. He lived in the greater Kansas City area for fifteen years before moving to Texas, where he is a professor in the creative writing program at the University of Houston.

Mary Jane Edwards

ANDRÉS RODRÍGUEZ is a native of Kansas City. He is the author of *Night Song* and *Book of the Heart*. In 2007 he won *Poets & Writers'* Maureen Egan Writers Exchange Award for Poetry. His poetry and prose have appeared in such journals as *Harvard Review, Drunken Boat, Cortland Review, Sagetrieb,* and *Palabra.*

David Joel

LINDA RODRIGUEZ is the author of *Every Last Secret*, winner of the Malice Domestic First Traditional Mystery Novel Competition, and two award-winning books of poetry, *Heart's Migration* and *Skin Hunger*. She has received the Midwestern Voices and Visions Award and the Elvira Cordero Cisneros Award. She is a member of Latino Writers Collective, Wordcraft Circle of Native American Writers and Storytellers, International Thriller Writers, and Sisters in Crime.

Todd Hanna

PHILIP STEPHENS is the author of a novel, *Miss Me When I'm Gone*, and a collection of poems, *The Determined Days*, which was a finalist for the PEN Center USA Literary Award. He lives in Kansas City.

Jarrett Mellenbruch

GRACE SUH is a writer and editor who lives in Kansas City. Her work has received awards from the Overbrook Foundation, the Edward F. Albee Foundation, the National Endowment for the Arts, the Djerassi Resident Artists Program, and the Ucross Foundation.

Bruce Carr

DANIEL WOODRELL is the author of *Winter's Bone* and seven other novels, most set in the Missouri Ozarks. His short story collection, *The Outlaw Album,* was published in 2011.